CHRISTMAS MIRACLES IN HOLLY WREATH

A SWEET CHRISTMAS BILLIONAIRE ROMANCE

RACHAEL ELIKER

ISBN 978-1-949876-23-9 (e-book)

ISBN 978-1-949876-24-6 (print)

Library of Congress Reference Number 1-8289540161

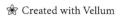 Created with Vellum

He insulted her. She slammed the door in his face. Only their mutual dislike of Christmas will bring them together.

Billionaire Ethan Wilder has a lot of reasons to hate Christmas, but being dumped by his cheating fiancée and ending up in Holly Wreath, Wyoming to hide out is currently the biggest. The next person on the receiving end of his bad attitude is the waitress serving him cold diner food.

Olivia Campbell hates waitressing but has to do something to pay the bills when customers at her bed and breakfast are slow. She puts on a happy face for her daughter, but after her husband walked out on them right before Christmas five years earlier, the season holds painful memories. To make matters worse, she opens her front door to discover her new houseguest is the cantankerous man from the diner with the gorgeous hazel eyes.

Living in close quarters should be unbearable, but as they share some of the simple pleasures of the holidays together,

Olivia and Ethan find themselves enjoying Christmas for the first time in a long time—but when Olivia discovers just who Ethan is, only a Christmas miracle may be what keeps them together.

GET YOUR FREE BOOK

Keep in touch with Rachael via her weekly newsletter, and receive your free book.

Visit www.RachaelEliker.com for details.

For my family, who are as wonderful as Christmas morning.

CHAPTER 1

E than would have rather been in the Maldives, digging his toes into the warm, soft sand of the beach, sipping on piña coladas while gentle waves rolled in from the Indian Ocean. Instead, he rested his forearms on the table and looked around the small diner in Middle-of-Nowhere, USA, and frowned. The décor was dated by at least two decades, and one of the fluorescent lights over his booth flickered, which didn't help his mood or his headache at all. But, if he tried to look on the bright side of his abysmal month, at least the diner was a warm retreat from the frosty outdoor temperatures. Snowflakes drifted from the clouds like they were in no hurry to touch down to the ground below, blanketing everything in soft white.

There were only a handful of other people in the diner. It was late—the sun had long since set, so when Ethan looked out the wall of windows next to his booth, he was met with his haunting reflection. He looked terrible. It'd been a day since he'd showered, and there were bags under his eyes that made him look older than he really was. Drawing in a ragged breath, he tried not to think of Mallory and how it was all her fault.

"Wishing you were in the tropics, too?"

Ethan looked up to the woman who had intruded into his thoughts. She was smiling kindly at him, but he didn't feel like reciprocating. He straightened the salt and pepper shaker and muttered, "That was the plan."

The waitress studied him with sparkling blue eyes that reminded him of the shallows of the Maldives. The soft pink uniform she wore was the same color as her cheeks, and though Ethan was sure she was inhaling calories all day from the smell alone of heavily fried food, the white apron tied around her waist emphasized she was trim and athletic. She had the appearance that she could hold her own despite her petite size. Her mouth twitched, like she wanted to laugh at what he'd said but had thought better of it.

"Weren't expecting to find yourself in Holly Wreath, were you? Wyoming isn't exactly everyone's idea of a tourist destination, but this little town is something else, especially around Christmas."

She pulled out a pen and a pad of paper, standing at the ready to take his order.

Ethan looked at her with incredulity. Anyone who could be so chipper working for an unimpressive place as a hole-in-the-wall diner in a town most people probably drove right through had to be deluding themselves. Or maybe he was just projecting his anger and disappointment over his fiancée onto her.

Ex fiancée.

"I'll have to take your word for it," Ethan said, avoiding looking her in the eye by studying the laminated menu in front of him. He ordered a hamburger and a large basket of onion rings with a strawberry milkshake.

"Road trip work up an appetite?" the waitress asked, taking his menu from him and tucking it under her arm.

"Apparently," he said.

She gave him another friendly smile, but he turned away, looking back at the shadow of his former self in the darkened window.

On one of the televisions hanging from the ceiling, the program caught his attention. A series of pictures of Mallory and Derek, one of his frat brothers from his undergraduate studies at Purdue University, flashed across the screen. They were laughing and playing on the beach, just like Ethan was supposed to be doing. His blood heated as he watched.

"Earlier this week, Mallory Janovich, fiancée of billionaire CEO Ethan Wilder, was seen enjoying herself in the Florida Keys with an unidentified man," a female entertainment journalist narrated as the slideshow of photos continued. "Ms. Janovich and Wilder had set a date for a spring wedding, but by the looks of things, the wedding is off."

"You think?" Ethan grumbled.

A closeup of Mallory and Derek kissing flashed onto the screen, and Ethan clenched his fists hard enough the whites of his knuckles showed.

"Keep your eyes open, ladies," the woman said. "That means Ethan Wilder is back on the market."

The series of photos ended with one the paparazzi had captured of Ethan leaving the office, talking on the phone and looking particularly grumpy. Glancing quickly around the restaurant, no one else seemed to notice Ethan was sitting among them. He was grateful for remaining anonymous, but he knew it would be difficult to stay that way if the media kept harrowing up his failed relationship by putting him on display.

Ethan's leg began to bounce up and down. He was trying to keep his thoughts from replaying over and over what had sent him stumbling into Holly Wreath in the first place, but he couldn't help it. Having Mallory run off with one of his friends only a few months before they were supposed to walk down the aisle was a blow to his confidence. He knew he wasn't perfect, but he was pretty sure he fulfilled every checkbox on Mallory's list—tall, dark, handsome, and rich. Sure, they sometimes butted heads, but every couple did. They'd always gotten over it because their match made sense. It didn't hurt either that Mallory's father owned a programming business that Ethan's company had been eyeing.

"Coming in hot," the waitress said, balancing her tray with a steady hand. Setting down his food, she pulled a straw from the pocket of her apron. "Need anything else? Ketchup? Extra napkins? A Christmas wish?"

Ethan raised an eyebrow at her. "A Christmas wish?"

She shrugged. "'Tis the season and all. You have to get requests in to Santa before he gets swamped. At least that's what I tell my daughter."

Ethan glanced at her nametag. *Olivia*. Taking the top off of his hamburger, he swirled a squirt of mustard onto the patty. "I haven't believed in Santa since I was four."

"Four? That's so young," Olivia said.

"Well, blame that on my parents dying in a car crash on their way home from a Christmas party," he said, meeting her eyes. "No amount of wishing or asking Santa brought them back."

He knew he was being dramatic, but telling people about his parents' death always brought conversation about Christmas to a screeching halt, and that's how he preferred it. He didn't care that people still celebrated the holiday as long as they didn't try to rope him into the silly traditions and false hopes a single day was supposed to bring.

Olivia's pretty eyes widened, and her mouth dropped open slightly. "I'm so sorry to hear. I didn't mean to—"

4

Ethan held up a hand. "It's fine. Not like you'd know it by looking at me."

Ethan straightened his tie, emphasizing the things she could draw conclusions from, like his expensive Italian-made suit, which anyone could see and know he was obviously well-off. He knew he was hiding behind a façade of wealth and indifference, but at the moment, it was the only thing he could do to cope.

"Well, if there's anything else you need, just holler. I'll be back to check on you in a few minutes."

"No need," Ethan said as he opened his napkin and laid it across his lap. "I don't need anything."

Olivia nodded and left to check on the few other customers and top off their waters, but he could feel her eyes on him. She had wanted to say something to him but had mercifully restrained herself. He wasn't in the mood to hash out his personal story with a total stranger, and it was taking all his self-restraint not to be any more of a jerk than he was already being.

His phone trilled in his breast pocket, and as he took it out, his heart hammered against his ribs while he checked to see who was calling. He half-expected it to be Mallory, calling to apologize for the ridiculous mistake she'd made. Ethan had always known Derek was a sly fox with a wandering eye. During college, he'd snatch up anything he could steal, even from supposed friends. It'd been funny when he'd stolen girlfriends from other guys in the fraternity when no one was seriously dating, but stealing Mallory, and from Ethan's sister's wedding, was a low blow as far as he was concerned.

Ethan groaned when he saw the name on the screen. "Emma."

He declined the call and put it face down on the table,

then picked up his hamburger. Mouth open and ready to take a bite, his phone started ringing again.

Ethan dropped his head and sighed, setting his hamburger back on his plate. Shoving an onion ring in his mouth and wiping the excess grease on his napkin, he picked up his phone. His sister wasn't going to leave him alone until he answered.

Swiping to answer, he said gruffly, "I'm in the middle of eating."

"Hello to you, too," Emma said without the least bit of offense.

"Is there something the matter? My hamburger is getting cold." Ethan poked at his burger and his frown deepened. "Well, col*der*."

"A hamburger?" Emma said. "Uh oh. Something really is the matter. You're the epitome of clean eating until you get upset, then you'd eat out of a dumpster if it made you feel better."

Ethan scrunched up his nose. "That's a complete exaggeration."

"Of course it is. But you have to admit, a hamburger is not on your usual diet."

Ethan glanced across the restaurant and spotted Olivia looking straight at him. She was drying coffee mugs and hanging them onto racks, obviously listening in on his conversation. The second his eyes locked onto hers, her cheeks flushed a deep red, and she looked down at what she was doing. Ethan was annoyed with himself that he noticed how cute she was when she was embarrassed.

Turning slightly in his booth to give himself at least a perceived measure of privacy, he avoided looking at his own reflection in the window. "Hamburgers are about all they have where I'm at."

"Where you're at?" Emma said. "You were supposed to be

leaving for the Maldives with Mallory today for your pre-wedding vacation."

Ethan let out another breath and pinched the bridge of his nose, hopelessly trying to stop the aching headache that was occupying itself right behind his eyes. All he wanted to do was finish his mediocre meal and head to the bed and breakfast where he'd rented a room and sleep until Christmas was over.

"You didn't hear?" he asked.

Emma's tone became solemn. "I had a feeling something was the matter. That's why I called. Our twin sense and all."

Despite himself, Ethan laughed. "Just because we're twins does doesn't mean we have a connected sixth sense."

"And just because you don't believe in it doesn't mean it's not real," Emma shot back. "Besides, stop trying to change the subject. Where are you?"

"I took a road trip."

"Mallory hates road trips."

"Yes, thank you. I know. I'm not with Mallory."

"What?" Emma gasped. "What's going on? Is something the matter with you two?"

Ethan scrubbed his hand down his face. "You could say that."

"So...explain."

"You haven't seen it on the news?"

"I just got back from my honeymoon, and though you think the world revolves around you, I don't keep tabs on my brother through television."

"Look, Emma..."

"If you don't tell me what's going on, I'm going to have to get nosy and start digging, and if I do that, I might discover some of your deep, dark secrets," Emma threatened.

Ethan let out a huff. "I highly doubt I have any secrets from my prying *older* sister."

"Watch it," Emma said with a warning tone. "I was only out of the womb two minutes before you, and I'll make you sorry if you keep teasing me about it."

"My apologies," Ethan said half-heartedly. Even teasing his sister wasn't making him feel any better. "If you must know, Mallory ran off with someone."

He had expected Emma to be shocked, but her calm, collected response was very telling. "With whom?"

"Derek," Ethan said, taking a sip of his too-sweet strawberry milkshake.

"Derek, as in your frat brother who was at my wedding?"

"The very one," Ethan confirmed. "Maybe this is all your fault."

"Me?" Emma said with a scoff. "How do you figure?"

"You're the one who invited him in the first place."

"First of all, he said he was going to be in town, and I thought you were friends. It was a last-minute decision since we had an extra space. Secondly, if Mallory dumping you and running off with the first guy she batted her eyes at was only a matter of Derek being invited or not, then your relationship was as steady as a sandcastle facing an incoming tide."

"Nice use of a metaphor," Ethan said. Emma was silent on the other end of the phone, and Ethan rolled his eyes. She was thinking something and was waiting for Ethan to ask. "Go ahead and say whatever it is you're going to say, Emma. You know you're going to share your wisdom whether I like it or not."

"Alright," Emma said confidently. "I never did like her, you know."

Ethan let out a bitter chuckle. "You're the one who introduced us."

"I introduced you because I was the one who knew who she was when you asked at that tech conference in San

Diego. I wasn't setting you up, just answering your question. You're the one who took it to the next level and started dating her."

"I wish you would've stopped me," Ethan said.

"I'm not sure you would've listened," Emma answered. "You always were one to look at your relationships like they were business transactions, and marrying Mallory logically made sense. With her family connections, it would've been a boon to our company. I mean, did you ever really love her?"

Ethan was surprised he had to stop and think. Sure, Mallory was beautiful and had a great sense of fun, highlighted by an infectious laugh, but having been forced to step back from the relationship when Mallory ditched him, Ethan struggled to remember any true spark between them.

"Yeah," Ethan said.

"Ha! You hesitated, and any man who's on the cusp of marrying the love of his life wouldn't answer so casually. I'm really sorry, Ethan. If it works out, you won't hear me say another word against Mallory, but if it doesn't..."

"You'll what?"

"I'll get a life-size cutout of Mallory, and we can throw darts at her," Emma said with a sinister laugh.

"You're pure evil, you know that?" Ethan said with a chuckle that eased the tension in his shoulders.

"Keeps life interesting," Emma said. "I just want to see you with someone who makes you happy and who you'll love the same way I love Rob."

Ethan sat back in his seat and draped his arm across the back of the booth. "We can't all be so lucky in love as you."

Ethan looked out the window, past his haunting reflection, and could see Christmas lights sparkling from a business across the street. Christmas had always been a difficult time of year for him, but Mallory dumping him was the cherry on top of this year's season. It might've been cynical, but he was starting to believe there really was no such thing as true love. It was about as real as Christmas miracles.

He looked back at his barely-eaten food and noticed a steaming mug of hot chocolate had been quietly set on a napkin while he'd been lost in his thoughts. Turning to see Olivia walk away, he held his hand over the receiver.

"Um, Olivia? I didn't order hot chocolate," he said, pointing to the mug.

"It's on the house," Olivia said with a close-lipped smile that still reached her eyes. "I made it myself and thought maybe you could use it."

Ethan gave her a curt nod. "Thanks."

He turned back around, but not before Olivia's smile grew until it looked like her cheeks might crack. Keeping straight-faced so no one would mistake him as cheerful, he returned to his phone call.

"Look, Emma. Mallory's off with Derek somewhere in Florida, probably soaking her cold feet in a hot tub with him for all I know. I'm fine, but since I was going to be gone anyway, I decided now was as good a time as any to go clear my head."

"Where are you?" Emma asked.

"It doesn't matter. All you need to know is that I'm safe, I haven't gone off the deep end, and I'll be working remotely, so you won't miss me one bit. Assuming, of course, this tiny town has any internet capabilities."

"So, my first clue is that you're in a small town?" Emma teased.

"Emma," Ethan groaned. "I'm not playing hide and seek with you."

"But I'm going to pretend you are. It's kind of important that the CEO of one of the biggest tech companies doesn't fall off the face of the earth without at least his sister knowing where he is."

Ethan begrudgingly took a sip of the hot chocolate, to show the waitress that her gesture wasn't totally unappreciated. When the warm drink hit his tongue, he was taken aback by how delicious it was. The food at the diner left a lot to be desired, especially compared to the places he was used to eating at, but the warm milk, rich chocolate, and frothy cream sprinkled with crushed peppermint was something else.

"Oh, wow," he mumbled to himself.

"What?" Emma asked.

"The waitress brought over a hot chocolate. I think it's the best I've ever had."

Emma snorted. "It's not like you have a particularly indulgent palate. I'm pretty sure you've been surviving on water, protein shakes, and kale since you were in college."

"Guess you'll have to take my word for it," Ethan said, taking another long draw of the hot chocolate, then licking the froth off his upper lip. "I think it has a dash of cinnamon in it."

"If you tell me where you are, I'll come try it for myself."

"Look, I'm a big boy, so you don't need to worry about me. I've got to go so I can grab some toiletries before the drugstore closes. I decided I needed a few days to clear my head, then I'll be back in the game. If anything comes up for work, shoot me an email."

He hung up without giving Emma a chance to say another word, supportive or otherwise. Ethan forced himself to take a few more bites of his food, saving the rest of the hot chocolate to wash it all down.

Standing up from the booth, he shrugged his leather jacket over his shoulders and pulled out his billfold, tossing a hundred-dollar bill down for Olivia. The hot chocolate had been worth it, and he appreciated her perceptiveness and patience with him. He'd been grumpy and she'd put up with him without so much as a sneer.

"How'd you enjoy your meal?" Olivia said, putting her hands on her waist. She smiled, and he almost hated to say it, but he believed in being honest, even if the truth hurt.

"It was fine. The burger was dry, while the onion rings were so greasy, I could use what's left over on my fingertips to style my hair." Olivia's rosy cheeks went pale. Grabbing the small suitcase, he'd hastily packed, he excused himself. "Sorry if that was a bit blunt. Honesty is the best policy and all."

Olivia drew herself to her full height—still a head and a half shorter than Ethan—and straightened her shoulders. "My apologies for the food. Our cook is new and is still learning the ropes."

"Well, you'd better teach them soon or you're going to lose tons of customers." Ethan strolled over to the door, holding onto the door handle but hesitating to open it. He couldn't bring himself to be so cold to a waitress he'd just met, no matter how angry he was at life. Tipping his head toward the empty mug of hot chocolate, he said, "That hot chocolate, though...if I had a Christmas wish, all I'd want would be another cup."

CHAPTER 2

The 1999 sedan Olivia drove struggled as she pulled into the driveway of the Holly Wreath Inn, dying before she'd reached her parking spot. Tipping her head forward and touching her forehead to the steering wheel, she couldn't decide if she should laugh or cry. Choosing neither, she put on the parking brake and left it where it was. She didn't have time to fight with her car.

Packing her things into her purse, she peered out the windshield at the Victorian mansion where she and her daughter, Heather, lived, and a swell of pride overtook her. They had decorated it for Christmas the weekend before, and contrasting against the enveloping darkness of the night sky, the home shone like a diamond. The dozens of strands of lights highlighted the interesting features of the house in a warm glow, creating a cozy feel that gave Olivia the warm fuzzies. She could see guests being in awe of the place as they arrived, and she'd be there to greet and invite them in to sit by a merrily crackling fire while they sipped the hot chocolate she'd whip up from her own secret recipe.

In the middle of her reverie, reality hit, and Olivia sighed.

The best part of the inn being decked out for Christmas was that no one would be able to see the crude roof patches Olivia had to do earlier in the autumn to stop a leak in the attic or that the old, tired house was in need of a new coat of paint. Shining with Christmas lights, the bed and breakfast could have fooled anyone into thinking it was flawless when really, it was as tired and beaten down as she was.

The happiness she felt wavered when she let her thoughts wander. She was bone weary from taking on a shift at the diner, and she still had so much to do: make up the bedroom for her one and only guest scheduled at the inn for the whole of December, sit down for a minute with Heather to see how her day had been before welcoming the guest who was scheduled to arrive at eight. When everyone else was all settled, she was going to try to get a jumpstart on breakfast, so she'd have something to feed her guest without having to get up at five in the morning to make it. If Olivia was anything, she definitely was *not* a morning person. When she'd awoken that morning, she'd pulled her violin out of the closet and set it in the corner, intending on playing some Christmas music to brighten the mood, but faced with overwhelming fatigue, she knew another day would pass without her rosining her bow.

Olivia opened her car door and stepped out into the cold, sinking her chin behind her scarf to keep warm. Walking up to the back door, she dropped her head and pinched her eyes shut, refusing to let the tears fall. She didn't want Heather to see her upset. Blowing out a breath, she steadied her emotions, stomped the snow off her feet, and let herself in.

"I'm home!" Olivia called as she opened the door.

She took off her coat and hung everything in one of the mudroom cubbies, rubbing her hands together to warm them up as she walked into the kitchen.

"Mom!"

Olivia barely turned the corner before Heather had her arms clamped around her mother's waist.

Kissing the top of Heather's head, Olivia hugged her daughter tightly, reminding herself that no tears were allowed until her head was on her pillow and after all the work was done.

"Mom, come, sit down," Heather said, towing Olivia by the hand to the large island in the center of the kitchen. It was one room that she'd already completely renovated, and she was glad for it. It was the beating heart of Holly Wreath and where most of the home's magic happened. "We baked cookies."

"Did you, now? I thought I smelled something delicious." Olivia smiled, meeting Twila's twinkling blue gray eyes. Twila, a grandmotherly woman from across the street had been Olivia's saving grace since she'd moved to Wyoming. Twila had taken Olivia under her wing when she'd arrived as a newlywed, helped her welcome Heather into the Holly Wreath Inn, been a shoulder to cry on when Olivia's husband walked away from it all...

"It's one of my favorites of my grandmother's recipes," Twila said, picking up one of the gingerbread men and making it dance. Olivia and Heather both laughed. "They remind me of being a little girl."

"That must have been a long time ago," Heather said without a second thought.

Olivia made a face at Heather. "That was rude."

"What?" Heather said. "It was, wasn't it?"

Twila chuckled, unoffended by Heather's inability to censor herself. "It was a long time ago, but sometimes it feels like it was only yesterday. I suppose Christmas does that to me. Transports me through time. It's part of the wonder of the season."

Tears stung at Olivia's eyes and threatened to betray her

tender emotions again. She hid them by going to the sink for a glass of water. Christmas had been so happy, but ever since her husband Jeff had left—choosing to walk out two days before Christmas—it was difficult to feel truly happy while he was always there in the back of her mind, dredging up a sadness she could never quite shake while the entire rest of the world was joyfully celebrating the season. It'd been five years already, and she put on a happy face for Heather, who barely remembered her absentee father, but sometimes, Olivia wondered if she'd ever be able to root out the sticky, persistent bitterness that was stuck deep in her soul.

"Can we decorate them tonight?" Heather asked with a slight whine to her tone.

Turning back around, Olivia produced a smile. "They do look pretty plain. But, you know the rules. Homework first."

"It's already done," Heather said, perking up in her seat. "Twila helped me finish. It was only one math sheet today."

"It took a mere five minutes when I finally peeled her eyes off the book she was reading," Twila said. "You've got a bookworm on your hands."

"Tell me about it," Olivia said, giving Heather a look that made her daughter simper sheepishly in return. "I've had to take more than one book away from her as a consequence for not doing something she was asked to do because she was lost in her own little world while reading."

Heather shrugged. "There could be worse things, right?"

"True," Olivia agreed.

"So? Can we decorate them? I promise to go to bed right when you tell me to. And we can put them out for the person who's coming to stay tonight. Please?"

Heather clasped her hands together and looked at Olivia with pleading, puppy dog eyes.

Olivia laughed at her daughter. "I don't know. I need to

get the master guest suite ready. It's been awhile since anyone's rented that room."

"Also already done," Heather said, holding up a pointer finger.

"We thought you might be too tired after working at the diner. It was Heather's idea," Twila said.

Heather listed everything they'd done on her fingers. "We dusted, put on clean sheets, swept, and wiped down the bathroom."

"Are there clean towels?" Olivia asked, folding her arms in mock sternness.

"And the mini bottles of shampoo and soap," Heather said, proudly pushing out her chest.

Stroking her fingers through Heather's silky brown hair she'd inherited from her mom, Olivia grinned. "You two have made my day. You and the last tip I got from the diner."

"Oh, really?" Twila asked. "Big tab?"

"No. And actually, he hated the food," Olivia said, letting herself laugh.

"*He*, huh?" Twila said as a smile twitched on her lips. "Was *he* handsome?"

"Twila!" Olivia said, tugging at the collar of her waitress uniform, which suddenly felt itchy and too hot.

Olivia knew there was no way she was going to be able to answer without backing herself into a corner. The man had been undeniably handsome, with hazel eyes that had depth to them, especially while he was smoldering and broody. He knew how to dress and groom, but he was *so* pompous that any virtue he might've had was overshadowed by his bad attitude. Olivia wasn't sure how anyone could put up with him, even if he was easy on the eyes, and as far as she was concerned, his only saving grace was that he'd been generous with his tip and had complimented her hot chocolate.

"What?" Twila said, shrugging. "It's an innocent enough

question. You're young and pretty and more than one man in this town has noticed you're unattached. Is it so wrong to want to see you settle down with someone who makes you happy?"

"I am happy," Olivia said. "I'm happy with Heather. She's my family. And so are you."

"Yeah, but what are you going to do when I grow up? I can't be seen with my mom when I'm at college," Heather said, wrinkling her freckled nose.

Olivia laughed, but it sounded forced. "Why are you all ganging up on me? Can't I be content with life the way it is, without a man?"

"Honey," Twila said, putting her hand over the top of Olivia's, "no one is trying to force anything on you, but you have to let go of the past and realize that one bad apple like you-know-who doesn't mean all men are rotten."

Olivia chose her words carefully. "I don't think all men are awful, but I know my heart is guarded because of Jeff."

"Letting someone have your heart is the biggest risk and reward love has to offer. When I think of the thirty years I had with my George, it was the most blessed time of my life. Having someone else to love doesn't mean you lose your identity or have less love for someone else. Love multiplies."

Olivia swallowed the lump of emotion that had lodged itself in her throat. "What if it's me? That I'm the one who's not lovable?"

Twila's expression softened, and Heather leaned her head against her mother's chest and hugged her again.

"Oh, Olivia," Twila said. "How a girl like you could ever think so little of herself is beyond me. You cook, you do your own home repairs, you play the violin like you were born with a bow in your hand, and you are the only one on the face of the planet who can make hot chocolate that would make any warm-blooded man fall to his knees and beg you to marry him. What's not to love?"

"I think you're exaggerating a bit," Olivia answered.

"If anything, I'm not being generous enough," Twila countered, looking at Olivia over the rims of her cherry red glasses.

"Besides," Olivia said, elbowing her grief and sadness to the back of her mind, "I highly doubt the guy at the diner is a potential suitor. I'm pretty certain he was just passing through."

"Regardless, you never said if he was handsome or not," Twila said.

"Well, Mom…" Heather wriggled her eyebrows. "Was he?"

Olivia caught her lower lip between her teeth, trying to figure out how to answer without completely incriminating herself. Despite his gruff manners, the man was certainly attractive.

"Yeah," she admitted with a stutter of schoolgirl giggling, "he was."

"And I'm assuming he wasn't married?" Twila said. "I'd hate to tarnish your reputation."

Olivia picked a fuzz off of her sweater and shrugged. "How would I know if he was married?"

"Don't tell me you didn't look to see if he was wearing a wedding band," Twila said with a measure of incredulity in her voice that made Olivia feel guilty for pretending she hadn't peeked.

"I didn't notice one, no," Olivia said.

"Maybe we should ask Santa to send you on a date for Christmas," Heather suggested. "It's been a while since you've gone out with anyone."

"Alright," Olivia laughed, clapping her hands and pointing to Heather's bedroom, off the kitchen and across the hall from her own. "I think it's time for you to get your pajamas on. If you want to decorate these cute little gingerbread people, I want you all ready to hop into bed when we're done."

Heather jumped off her seat and gave Twila a peck on the cheek and squeeze goodbye.

"Thanks for hanging out with an old hen like me," Twila said.

"See you tomorrow," Heather said, twiddling her fingers and disappearing into her room.

Taking her winter coat off the back of one of the chairs, Twila slipped her arms in and arranged her scarf before she zipped it all the way to the top.

Looking past Olivia to see if Heather was listening in, Twila leaned in and lowered her voice. "There's something you should know."

"Oh?"

"Heather was asking me about Santa Claus today."

"Yeah? What'd she say?"

"I think she's beginning to believe he's, you know..." Twila rolled her hands in front of her, trying to find the right words. "A part of Christmas lore."

Olivia sighed, her insides deflating a little bit more than they already were. "I'm not surprised. She keeps reminding me that she's not a child anymore. I kind of wish she still was."

"What do you mean?" Twila cocked her head to the side. "One of the joys of parenthood is watching your children grow."

"I know," Olivia muttered. "I guess I want to keep her oblivious to the pain of life, and believing that Santa would remember her enough to bring her presents even when her own father had walked out on her has been one way I felt I could give her a happy childhood. Without a belief in Santa, I'm not sure what I can do to buffer things for Heather."

"I think you're overthinking it."

"Am I?" Olivia said, massaging her temples with one hand. "I don't want her to miss out on anything because she's being raised by a single mom."

"And she won't. You're doing the best you can with the situation you're in. Kids are resilient. And you know what? Even with the best parents, children grow up and figure out…" Twila paused and looked behind Olivia again, "that Santa isn't real."

"I wasn't ready for it, I guess. That wide-eyed wonder of children is one of the best parts of Christmas."

"It happens to everyone, sooner or later. I don't think any of the amazement of Christmas has to be lost, just because a belief in Santa is out of the equation."

"How did you break it to your boys?" Olivia asked as she ambled to the back door with Twila.

"Oh, they were horrible snoops. Caught George and me putting presents under the tree when they were six and eight. Served them right as far as I'm concerned."

Olivia laughed with her. "Thanks for watching Heather today. You're an angel."

"Oh, pish posh," Twila said, batting her hand in the air. "I think I need time with Heather as much as she needs me. She has a way of making me feel like a carefree kid again."

"That's funny. Sometimes it feels like she's the responsible adult around here."

"She's a great girl," Twila said. "You're raising her right."

"She's a gem," Olivia agreed.

Twila reached for the door but stopped herself. "Don't you forget what I said."

Olivia's eyes shifted back and forth. "About what?"

Twila bumped Olivia's arm playfully. "That you don't have to shield yourself from love. Heather wants to see you happy, too. You don't need to feel like a failure because the

21

man you fell in love with first flaked on you and Heather. There are a lot of good guys out there. Let your happiness grow if someone special comes along. Promise me that."

Olivia held up her hand, teasing Twila as she pretended to make a solemn oath. "I promise if the right guy falls right into my lap, I won't immediately chase him out the door."

"You'll thank me for it later," Twila assured.

"Don't get ahead of yourself. I think I've dated every eligible bachelor in Holly Wreath, and I can assure you, none of them qualified as Mr. Right."

Twila stepped out into the cold. "Good thing you run a beautiful bed and breakfast and get all sorts of interesting people passing through your house."

Olivia knew she was never going to win against Twila. Rolling her eyes and folding her arms as she leaned against the door jamb, Olivia waved goodbye to her friend.

Olivia shut and deadbolted the back door, and Heather slid into the kitchen on her socks, grabbing the piping bags of frosting that were lying next to the sink. While Olivia got down her cookie decorating supplies, Heather talked her ear off, barely stopping to take a breath, and together, they decorated all two dozen of the gingerbread men.

Wiping up the stray candies and globs of frosting, Olivia pulled out a beautiful silver platter she'd been handed down from her aunt, and Heather arranged eight of the best cookies so each of their smiling faces were showing.

"There," Heather said with satisfaction as she brushed her hands together. "If a plateful of gingerbread cookies doesn't scream Christmas, I don't know what would."

"It's very festive," Olivia agreed. "I'll be sure to offer one to our guest, whenever they arrive."

"Who's coming to stay?" Heather asked, hopping off her chair and leaning against the back of it.

"I don't really know. A lady called today and just gave a

last name. Wilder. Said they'd be arriving about eight in the evening."

Heather craned her neck to look at the clock on the stove. "It's already nine."

Panic wormed its way through Olivia's chest. Yes, there would be a small cancelation fee if they didn't show, but it wouldn't even put a dent in the heating bill of the Holly Wreath Inn. That would mean Olivia would have to take more shifts at the diner, and if business didn't pick up soon, she might have to look for a second job just to pay the mortgage.

"Nine, huh?" Olivia said. "That means you're already half an hour late for bed. Now scoot. And don't forget to say your prayers."

Olivia started stacking the clean dishes on the counter to put them away and silently said a prayer of her own.

Dear Lord, I could really use a Christmas miracle right about now. If you're not too busy—

The soft chime of the doorbell interrupted Olivia's impromptu prayer, and her heart leapt at the sound.

"*Ooo!*" Heather squealed, "That must be them."

Excitement zipped through Olivia's chest. "I can't imagine there are too many other people who'd be ringing our doorbell this late."

"I'll get it," Heather offered.

Catching her daughter by the elbow, she said, "You know that's another house rule. The first time, I get to answer the door. You know. To make sure they're not a creep."

Heather sassed her mom by crossing her eyes, which only made Olivia chuckle. "You'd better go get it then before they change their mind."

"I will. I want to take a quick peek in the mirror to check myself to make sure I don't have frosting all over my face."

"You look fine, Mom."

Olivia hurried across the kitchen to a small mirror she'd hung by the back door and fussed with a small, persistent curl that grew at the base of her neck despite the rest of her hair being stick straight. "You've said that before, and I've gone out with dried drywall putty smeared on my forehead. I felt like such an idiot when the lady at the hardware store pointed it out to me."

Heather shrugged. "I'm so used to seeing you with paint under your nails and grease on your face all the time anyway. Now, if you're not going to answer the door, I am."

"Alright," Olivia said, wrinkling her nose and grinning as she grabbed the platter of gingerbread cookies and set them on a small table just off the entryway. Through the frosted glass of the front door, she could barely make out anything definite about her guest, other than they were a broad-shouldered, towering man.

Taking a deep breath, she put a welcoming smile on her face and swung open the front door.

"Welcome to the Holly—"

The words caught in her throat when she realized who it was. Staring back at her was the rude man from the restaurant, who regarded her with the kind of amusement that a crocodile would look at another animal right before he ate it up.

"Hello, Olivia," he said with a smirk. "It seems we meet again."

CHAPTER 3

It took all of Ethan's resolve not to let the smirk he felt coming on spread across his entire face. He was just as surprised to see Olivia behind the open door as he was to be standing on her porch. She narrowed her eyes at him before she slammed the door in his face hard enough that the wreath on the front door wobbled and fell off.

He took a step back, surprised at Olivia's audacity. He couldn't think of the last time anyone had been so brazen as to shut him out of anything. Of course, that was because everyone else he interacted with knew exactly who he was. Still, her reaction did bring on a wave of guilt about how he'd treated her at the diner. He'd been more cruel than he'd led himself to believe. Though he stood by his assessment of the low-quality food, he admitted to himself that he could have been more diplomatic in how he'd said it. She wasn't the one cooking, and she certainly wasn't the one who'd put him in the mood he was in.

He could hear muffled whispers behind the door, and he stooped over so he could hear better, pretending he was only helping by picking up the dislodged wreath.

"What are you doing? He's a paying guest!" hissed one voice—a young girl by his guess.

Olivia answered, "I know, but I don't know if I can put up with the likes of someone like him for a week. I already had one Christmas ruined by a man, and I don't need another one putting a damper on it."

"You've met him before?"

"Unfortunately."

"Is it...?"

"The guy from the diner, yes. I was right that he was traveling, but I didn't put two and two together that he was the one coming to stay here. My brain is crispier than fried chicken." Olivia sighed heavily enough that Ethan could visualize her shoulders slumping.

Ethan scrubbed his hand down his face. If Emma ever found out how he'd treated Olivia, she'd never let him live it down. It wouldn't matter that Olivia had been a stranger at the time and he had thought he'd never see her again. Emma had a moral compass that never wavered.

"Mom," said the girl, "you can do this. Put a smile on your face and pretend like you've never met him before, if that's what it takes. We need his business. The roof needs to be replaced, the deck is starting to rot, and someday, I'd like to have something other than bare subflooring in my bedroom."

Eyeing his BMW that he'd parked in the driveway, he seriously considered slinking back to it and finding a nearby shopping center where he could park his car and sleep until he was awake enough to drive to the next town. He'd been the epitome of a snobby rich dude, and his only consolation for his behavior was that he'd been generous with his tip. For all he knew, Olivia thought he was flaunting his money in her face.

Before he could move, the door swung open, and he blinked against the bright lights flooding out the door. He looked up at a girl that couldn't have been older than eight but was very distinctly Olivia's child. She had the same spread of delicate freckles across her nose and cheeks, the same glossy brunette hair and heart shaped face, but instead of striking blue eyes like her mother, hers were rich and earthy brown.

Her smile was welcoming if a bit sly, and she planted her hands on her hips. "You must be Mr. Wilder. Please, come in."

Ethan's gaze slipped behind the girl to where Olivia was watching him, looking a shade paler. Swallowing and forcing her mouth into a smile, her eyes were still a mixture of anger, distrust, and desperation.

"Yes," Olivia said. "Please, come in."

Standing up to his full height, Ethan handed over the wreath. "This fell off."

The girl laughed like he'd told a great joke and took it from him, hanging it back on the door before tugging him inside. "Don't worry about it. That old thing is always falling off."

"It's a good thing you have a sturdy front door," Ethan quipped straight-faced. His joke was lost on Olivia, who maintained as pleasant an expression as she could.

"We're happy to have you, Mr. Wilder," Olivia said stiffly.

"Please. Ethan will do."

"I'm Heather," the girl said, pointing her thumb at her chest. "It sounds like you've already met my mom."

"Briefly," Olivia said, running her hands down the front of her vintage-looking floral apron she was wearing over her waitressing uniform. Holding out her hand in a gesture of goodwill, she said, "Nice to meet you Ethan Wilder."

Ethan adjusted the shoulder strap of his laptop case, firmly shaking her hand and hoping she wouldn't put together that he was *the* Ethan Wilder, CEO of Wilder Tech.

It didn't appear Olivia had seen the entertainment news clip on the television at the diner, so unless she'd picked up a recent copy of *Forbes* magazine, the only other place he could think he'd being featured recently, he might be able to get away with anonymity hiding out in her bed and breakfast.

Olivia ran her hands down her front again, making sure she was presentable, she said, "Let's get you warmed up and settled in."

Olivia turned her back and walked to a coat closet built under the stairs while Heather trotted over to a table to pick up a platter of gingerbread cookies. Ethan kept his face neutral as he soaked in his new surroundings. The warmth inside was a welcome relief from the relentless, biting cold that had pressed on him nonstop since he had pulled into Holly Wreath. The house smelled of spice, oiled wood, and Olivia's perfume, a perfect combination that gave it a homey feel. The space itself was impeccably clean if a bit tired and worn. He made sure not to stare at the crack in the plaster by the sitting room chandelier too long. Ethan was well aware that Olivia's eyes were on him again.

"Quite the place you have here," he said, setting down his few belongings.

"Thank you," Olivia said, her eyes running across the home with an appraising glance.

"It was one of the first homes built in Holly Wreath," Heather said. "It's technically a mansion." Olivia gave her daughter a look, but Heather didn't seem to notice.

"I thought so," Ethan said.

"Cookie? I baked them, and my mom helped decorate them," Heather said proudly, thrusting the platter toward him.

Sure she wasn't going to take no for an answer, he picked one up and nibbled at an arm. The cookie was chewy and rich with spices, and though gingerbread wasn't his favorite, it was delicious enough to make him reconsider.

"Oh, wow," he said, taking a heartier bite. "That's really good."

"You sound surprised," Olivia said, shifting on her feet.

"Is it because the food at the diner is gross?" Heather asked, making Ethan choke on his cookie. He could feel his cheeks growing warmer as Olivia raised her eyebrows, expectantly awaiting his answer. "Just so you know, my mom may work at the diner once in a while, but she's not the one cooking. She'll feed you really, really well when you're here. Promise."

"I'm looking forward to it," Ethan said.

Holding his cookie between his teeth, he pulled out his wallet and counted out a few hundred-dollar bills and handed them over. "My secretary told me she arranged for me to pay in cash. Is that enough to cover the cost?"

Heather's eyes widened, and she glanced over at her mom. Olivia didn't reach for it. "I don't keep any change at the house. At least not that much."

"Then keep the change," he said.

Olivia's lips pursed and pulled into a slight frown. "I appreciate the gesture, but you're offering me over twice the amount it costs to stay here. Our inn may be...humble, but we aren't in need of charity."

"I'm not trying to imply anything other than my gratitude that I was able to find a place to stay so last minute. Consider it a token of appreciation. I insist."

Refusing to back down, Ethan didn't budge, but neither did Olivia. Seeing an opportunity, Heather snatched the money from his hand and folded it in half, then tucked it into Olivia's apron pocket. "How about my mom keeps it, and when she gets a chance, she can get your change. Or maybe you'll decide to stay longer, and it'll all even out. Deal?"

"Sounds like a plan to me," Ethan agreed, taking another bite of the gingerbread man. "As long as it's alright with your mother."

"As you wish," Olivia said, brushing a wisp of loose hair out of her eyes and back behind her ear. Taking his coat out of his hands, she draped it over the hanger and tucked it into the closet. "Can I show you to your room? I'm sure you're tired from traveling."

"What makes you think I'm not from around these parts?" Ethan said, raising a teasing eyebrow at her.

Olivia's eyes darted to his. "I've lived in Wyoming long enough to know there isn't anyone within a two-hundred-mile radius that's rich enough to have a secretary call and make a reservation for them. That means you drove at least a couple of hours to get here."

"Very astute." Ethan said, finishing off the cookie with one large bite. Emma was right that he'd gone off the deep end, eating all kinds of stuff he usually avoided, but the spiciness and warmth of the cookie and the way it melted in his mouth was too much to resist.

"It's also because I'm pretty sure you'd be famous if you lived here," Heather said.

"Oh, really?" Ethan said, tucking one of his hands into the pocket of his pants, hoping no one noticed the tightness of his expression at the mention of people recognizing him. "Why's that?"

"Because you're really handsome. I think you'd get a reputation around town, and everyone would know you as that handsome fella," Heather answered with an ear to ear grin.

Olivia rolled her eyes and turned her back, though Ethan didn't miss that her cheeks were glowing and pink. Had Olivia thought he was attractive? Shutting the closet door,

Olivia looked to Heather. "Alright, missy. I think it's time for you to go to bed."

Heather didn't grumble as she hugged her mom goodnight and waved at Ethan. "Sleep tight, Ethan. You're going to enjoy your stay here. Everybody does."

"It'll be a nice break from reality," Ethan said.

Heather skipped down the hall toward the kitchen and out of sight. Olivia blew out a breath and apologized. "Sorry if she put you on the spot. She really enjoys meeting new people, but sometimes, I can't get her to filter herself. If the idea pops into her brain, it's coming right out of her mouth whether people want to hear it or not."

"Sounds a lot like me," Ethan said.

Olivia's clear blue eyes met his, and she cracked a small grin. "I suppose. Let's get you upstairs to your room. You look like you might fall asleep on your feet, and after the day I've had, I'm not hoisting you up the stairs."

Ethan ran his fingers through his hair, then down his face. "Is it that obvious? That I'm exhausted?"

"You look plum tuckered," Olivia said, taking his suitcase and carrying it up the beautiful mahogany staircase that creaked and groaned, like it had a story to tell with every step. "Bad day?"

"Bad month," Ethan muttered.

Olivia stopped and looked over her shoulder at him. "I'm sorry to hear."

"Thanks," Ethan said, avoiding her eyes. "I'm not a big fan of Christmas to begin with."

"I can sympathize," Olivia said, finishing up the steps and taking a sharp left down the hallway. "Nothing that a good night's sleep won't put into perspective."

Ethan almost asked about her distaste for Christmas and who the other man was who'd ruined it for her, but he caught himself. He didn't want her to know he'd been eavesdropping through the door because frankly, it was none of his business.

"That's true. I always feel better after I've had a good eight hours," Ethan said.

Olivia stopped at the first door and swung it open, gesturing for him to enter. The king bed at the center of the spacious room was covered with a simple duvet with half a dozen throw pillows carefully arranged to add depth and an artistic touch. A matching dresser set in cherry wood had been polished until it shone, and the décor was tasteful yet interesting. It certainly wasn't the fanciest place he'd ever stayed, but the unspoken charm of it made him feel like he was going home.

"The bathroom is just off to the left. There are toiletries in the shower if you need them, and holler if you'd like more towels," Olivia said.

She handed over his suitcase, and her fingers brushed against his. He noticed she avoided his gaze as a tinge of red blossomed in her cheeks. Olivia studied her feet, then glanced up to meet his eyes. Clamping her lips, she curved her fingers behind her ear to secure a loose lock of hair, then spun on her heels to leave.

"Thanks for the hot chocolate," Ethan blurted. Olivia stopped at the top of the stairs, her hand resting on an ornately carved newel post. "At the diner. It really hit the spot." He forced himself to stop before he began rambling.

Amusement danced in her eyes. "You're welcome. You looked like you could use it."

"It was delicious. I did mean it when I said it was one of the best things I've ever had."

Olivia's mouth quirked into a smile that made Ethan's heart do a funny little flip in his chest. "Of course it was. It was my secret recipe."

Ethan laughed. "Does that mean I shouldn't bother asking for a recipe to send to my sister?"

Olivia folded her arms across her chest and chuckled lightly. "Even if I gave you the recipe, it wouldn't come out right. So yeah, don't bother asking."

"Wow," Ethan said, leaning his shoulder against the wall, "it's been a while since anyone's shot me down so fast."

Olivia undid her arms and shrugged, taking the first step down the staircase. "I know how much you like honesty."

Ethan smiled, and Olivia returned it with a taunting little smirk of her own. He was sure he was flirting with a waitress he'd only met and insulted a few hours earlier, the whole time wishing he hadn't have been so blunt with his criticism. He didn't know if it was the house or the sweet gingerbread that embodied the taste of Christmas or Olivia herself, but the sting of Mallory's betrayal was little more than an afterthought ever since he entered Holly Wreath Inn.

"Breakfast will be ready whenever you are. Any time after seven." Taking another two steps down, Olivia stopped briefly and looked at him between the balusters. "Sweet dreams, Ethan Wilder."

CHAPTER 4

"What am I doing?" Olivia muttered to herself as she punched down a pillowy mound of sweet bread dough and turned it onto the floured countertop.

The soulful strains of *What Child is This?* drifted out through her phone's speaker and made her feel like the kitchen wasn't quite so empty. She kept it quiet enough that she wouldn't wake up Heather or bother Ethan, but loud enough that it seemed she was speaking to a friend, rather than herself.

She pushed her knuckles into the dough that she was going to turn into cinnamon rolls and began leaning her weight into it. She'd meant to start the rolls the night before but Ethan showing up on her doorstep had thrown her whole evening off, and instead of being a responsible adult, she'd blown off her to-do list. After she'd shown him to his bedroom and made sure he was settled, she went right down to her room, grabbing a bag of chocolates she had stashed in the pantry on her way, and flipped to the first thing she found even slightly entertaining on her bedroom television.

She was invested enough in the movie by the time she realized it was a holiday romance that she couldn't turn it off. Olivia rolled her eyes at herself, getting sucked into a fictitious love story while eating chocolate and trying desperately to keep her mind off Ethan and the way he made butterflies flutter in her stomach while simultaneously making her want to tear her hair out because of his broody, haughty personality. Why did the man that irritated her have to be so frustratingly attractive?

When the movie couple got their happily ever after, and the credits rolled at eleven thirty, Olivia still wasn't ready to go to bed. Her mind was reeling, wondering how she was going to endure an entire week of Ethan staying at her bed and breakfast. It wasn't so much that he could be irritating and gruff—she'd dealt with enough difficult customers in her time with the Holly Wreath Inn that were rough around the edges when they arrived due to the stress of life. They'd always left much pleasanter people with a few days of quiet, homey living. It was that she knew she'd felt something for him, and no matter what she'd promised Twila, that scared her.

Instead of lying down to sleep like she knew she should, Olivia had rosined up her bow and played her violin until after midnight. Heather had reassured her that she was basically dead to the world when she was asleep, and Olivia was certain Ethan wasn't going to hear her. The house was big, and the doors were solid. The melodic strains of music were a balm to her tattered nerves at the end of a very trying day. When her alarm rang at five the next morning so she could get breakfast ready in time, she regretted burning the midnight oil as she tried to rub sleep from her eyes and got ready.

Pulling a rolling pin out of a drawer, Olivia shaped the dough into a long rectangle and continued to scold herself.

"You're not allowed to pine over the guests. It's totally inappropriate."

She grabbed a stick of softened butter and spread it over the entire length of the dough, then generously sprinkled the entire thing with cinnamon and brown sugar. Blinking a few times to try and stave off the drowsiness that made her eyelids feel like lead weights, she carefully rolled up the dough and pinched shut the seams.

Olivia hummed along with the music while she worked to keep herself awake. Rummaging through her drawers, she took out the package of dental floss she kept in the back of the measuring cup drawer and marked out sixteen even rolls. It was more than she was going to need, but it wouldn't be difficult to find people to give them to so they wouldn't go to waste.

"Is that floss?"

Olivia yelped and banged her hip into the counter as she jumped back, holding her hand over her racing heart. Ethan stood in the doorway with his hands in the pockets of his jeans and looked delighted he'd caught her off-guard. Olivia ignored that the way he looked at her made her knees go weak.

"You scared me," Olivia said, taking a deep breath to calm herself, trying not to glower at him.

Ethan's boyish smile widened. "So it seems. Sorry. I wasn't trying to be sneaky."

Olivia looked at the clock above the sink. "It's only six. I wasn't expecting you downstairs for at least another hour."

Ethan took her conversing with him as an invitation, and he strolled further into the kitchen. "I fell asleep about five seconds after I laid down in bed. Nine thirty to five thirty was a full eight hours."

"Eight hours?" Olivia said. "Really indulging yourself, aren't you? Most people who come to stay here at least let themselves sleep until the sunlight starts cracking over the horizon."

Ethan chuckled, and Olivia was keenly aware how closely he stood behind her. She could smell the fresh smell of soap on his warm skin, while his hair was still damp and slightly curled from his shower.

"I haven't had eight hours of sleep in ages. Usually I'm lucky to be running on five."

Olivia clucked her tongue. "Running on about five myself, I really don't think that's healthy. I can barely keep my eyes straight."

Ethan laughed again and stepped over to the counter, leaning against it and stretching his legs out, crossing one ankle over the other. Olivia's gaze trailed over to his sinewy forearms and how his muscles moved as he gripped the edge of the counter. She quickly gained control of her wandering vision and forced her focus back to the mess of flour she was cleaning up while she let the cinnamon rolls rise, but not before she was sure Ethan had caught her gawking.

Olivia spoke, hoping it would keep Ethan from thinking Olivia meant anything by admiring how trim and fit he was. "To answer your question, yes, I use dental floss to make my cinnamon rolls. When you wrap it around the dough and pull it together, it cuts it cleanly without squashing anything." She held up a cinnamon roll to show him before she put it on the pan. "See? Perfect."

"Huh," Ethan said. "That's clever."

"I'd take credit for it, but I learned it by making them with my mom. She was a regular Martha Stewart."

"That must've been nice to learn that kind of stuff from her," Ethan said.

Olivia nodded and blew a strand of hair off her forehead. "It was. I never wanted for any fresh baked goodies."

A silence fell over the kitchen, and Olivia wasn't sure how

to remedy it, other than keeping busy. She didn't know Ethan well enough to feel comfortable in the quiet, and something about him watching her tidy up the kitchen made her wary. Most of her guests kept to their room or the front of the house, where there was a small library, a dining room, and a living room where she'd started a small fire in the wood burning stove. Coming into the kitchen almost felt like breaking into her personal space.

Olivia grabbed a broom off a hook in the mud room and swept up what flour had scattered on the floor. Standing up straight, her hand was trembling as she balanced the broom on its bristles. "I was meaning to apologize."

"About what?" Ethan helped himself to a handful of assorted nuts from a decorative glass dish Olivia had planned to set out.

"Slamming the door in your face last night."

"Oh. Right. That." Ethan laughed like it was all a good joke, and Olivia couldn't help but feel flush. "It wasn't the kind of welcome I was expecting."

"It was…I had a long day."

"I don't suppose my assessment of the diner food helped your opinion of me much."

Olivia moved to dump the dustpan and return the broom. "All I do is waitress there. I know it's no five-star restaurant."

"You're right. It's not." Olivia rolled her eyes while her back was turned to him. "But, I do think I was a bit harsh. To be honest, I was having a less than stellar day, too."

"Fair enough," Olivia said as she squeezed out a dish cloth and finished wiping off the counter. She tossed the dishcloth into the sudsy water and wiped her hands dry on her apron, then held her hand out to shake his. "Truce?"

Ethan put his hand in hers and a heat crept up Olivia's arm and radiated through the rest of her, the way a mug of her hot chocolate could warm her down to her toes with one sip. She liked the way her hand fit in his and the way his eyes crinkled at the corners when he grinned, which grew more pronounced the longer she stared. Olivia snapped out of it when she heard a gentle rapping at the back door.

Pulling her hand away, she wiped her hands off again, like it would get rid of the surprising sensation Ethan had caused. Walking over through the mudroom to the rear entrance, she turned on the outside light and saw Twila dancing from one foot to the other, trying to keep warm.

Undoing the deadbolt, Olivia threw open the door and tugged Twila inside, slamming it just as fast to keep the unrelenting frigid air out. "What are you doing here so early? It can't be more than twenty-five degrees outside."

"It's only twenty-two," Twila said, taking off her earmuffs and blowing warm air onto her fingers. "If we're lucky, we might break above freezing today, though I'm not holding out hope if the merciless wind doesn't knock it off."

Olivia took Twila's coat from her and hung it on one of the hooks. "And you thought it'd be a good idea to take a stroll in the pre-dawn tundra?"

"I saw your light was on, so I knew you were up. I came over to check out your new guest. To see who he is and if he's handsome."

Dread seeped through Olivia's veins, and she didn't want to go back into the kitchen to see the mischievous smirk on Ethan's face because there was no way he'd missed what Twila had said.

Olivia tightened her lips and gave Twila a pointed look that Twila couldn't miss. Smacking her hand to her forehead, Twila said in a loud whisper, "He heard me, didn't he?"

Olivia nodded, itching at the beads of sweat that were seeping out along her hairline.

Stepping around Olivia, Twila went into the kitchen first with her head held high, while Olivia couldn't seem to shrug off the tension that gathered in her neck and shoulders. "Good morning," she said to Ethan. "Nice to meet you. I'm Twila Birch. I live across the street."

Ethan looked to Olivia, and sure enough, there was that haughty smile that was so polarizing. "Pleasure to meet you, Twila. I'm Ethan."

"I guess seeing you answers my question," Twila said, patting the back of his hand while she shook it. "You certainly are a looker, aren't you?"

"Twila," Olivia said. "I'm not sure my guest wants to be...*appraised*."

"It's alright," Ethan said as he chuckled. "Nothing like a little boost to the ego first thing in the morning."

He winked at Twila, and her grin widened before it disappeared completely. Twila narrowed her eyes at him and tapped a finger on her chin. "Do I know you? I have the strangest feeling we've met before."

Ethan's expression morphed momentarily, and Olivia could have sworn it looked like something akin to alarm, but he quickly got it under control. "I think I'd remember a town like Holly Wreath and a lady like you, Twila."

"You're right. You have one of those handsome faces that's on every men's cologne ad in those magazines they sell in the grocery checkout line," Twila said, patting him on the cheek. "So, what brings you to our neck of the woods anyway? Holly Wreath is a place like no other, but isn't exactly a prime vacation destination, especially when it's..." She rolled her hand in the air, searching for the right word.

"Frigid?" Ethan offered.

"Right. Other than our annual Christmas festival, Holly Wreath is your typical sleepy small town most of the year," Twila said.

Ethan crossed his arms and tilted his head back and forth

as he tried to figure out how to answer. "I needed a little break from reality."

Twila planted her hands on her hips. "Then you came to the right place. Olivia will take good care of you."

"I'm sure she will," Ethan said. "Although I might have to let out my pants if she keeps feeding me so well."

Twila tipped her head back and let out a peal of laughter. "You've got that right. She can cook me under the table, and I've got a good thirty-three years on her."

"You're being modest, Twila. A lot of what I've learned I picked up from you, you know," Olivia said. Tossing her head in Twila's direction, Olivia told Ethan, "If you don't like how much butter and sugar I use in my cooking and baking, you can blame her."

"Well, excuse me, missy," Twila sassed. "It's not like my family handed down a lot of salad recipes that I could share with you."

Twila looked at Olivia, and they both started laughing. Ethan shrugged. "Guess I'll have to track down the gym. You have one, I assume?"

"There's only one, and it's not exactly busy this time of year," Twila said, wiping away a tear from the corner of her eyes. Clapping her hands and rubbing them together, she said, "Well. Now that the mystery of who your guest is has been solved, I actually came over to ask something."

"Why do I have a feeling that I'm going to regret this?" Olivia asked. Olivia peeked under the tea towel she'd laid over the cinnamon rolls while they rose. They were puffing up nicely, so she turned on the oven, ignoring that Ethan's eyes followed her everywhere she went.

"And I thought we were friends," Twila said, feigning hurt.

"We are, but you have a way of making me regret saying

yes to you more often than I'd like to admit," Olivia said with a smirk.

Twila tsked. "If it makes you feel better, I wasn't going to ask you."

Olivia stood up straight. "Who...?"

She followed Twila's gaze over to Ethan, who looked like he wasn't sure what to make of the twinkle in Twila's eyes.

"Twila," Olivia warned. "He's here on vacation, not to indulge you in one of your harebrained schemes."

"It's nothing like that," Twila said. "All I was going to ask was if he'd be able to help me decorate Main Street."

Ethan's brow furrowed. "What for?"

Twila's face brightened. "For the festival, of course. It's the most magical time in Holly Wreath, aside from Christmas, mind you, and everything needs to be just so."

"I'm sure it does," Ethan said.

Something in the way he answered irked Olivia. Resting one hand on her waist, she said, "It might be a forgettable, small-town hoedown compared to wherever you're from, but it really is something special."

From the hallway, Heather shuffled into the kitchen, bleary-eyed and yawning. She was dressed for school, but her hair was a tangled mess from sleeping. "What's all the bickering going on out here?"

"We're not bickering," Olivia said, waving her hand for Heather to come over so she could help tame her hair. "We were discussing how great the festival is."

"If it's so great, then why aren't you helping?" Ethan asked, raising his eyebrows.

Olivia felt silly giving her answer. "I'm busy. Lots to do around the inn that I've been putting off."

"I see," Ethan said.

Olivia turned her back to him, flipped on the oven light,

and peered inside. "I thought the ladies in your bridge club were helping you pull it together, Twila."

"Oh," Twila said, batting her hand in the air. "You know how they are. They're so...*old*. I need some fresh blood to keep things from getting stale. Besides, none of them are brave enough to climb up ladders, and even if they were, they would break a hip for sure if they fell."

Twila watched Ethan, her eyes brimful of hope when Olivia cut in. "Don't feel like you need to indulge her. You're here on vacation, and you don't need to be roped into something you don't want to do. It wouldn't be right."

Ethan rubbed a finger across his lips, and Olivia couldn't help but stare at his mouth.

Heather perked up, and she wagged her pointer finger in the air. "I have an idea."

"What is it, honey?" Twila said. "I'm open to suggestions."

"Actually, it was for Mom," Heather said while her eyes trailed over to Ethan. "And him."

Twila's eyebrows shot up her forehead and her eyes danced between Olivia and Ethan. Holding back a heavy sigh, Olivia asked, "Well? What is it?"

"If Ethan helps you with some of the projects around the house, you and Ethan will have time to help Twila with the festival," Heather said. "It'll be a win-win-win for everyone."

Olivia shifted on her feet and ground her teeth. She'd put herself between a rock and a hard place without a way to escape, and Ethan was watching her to see what her answer was going to be. "I don't know. Do you know how to run a saw without cutting your fingers off?"

"I've never cut a piece of wood in my life," Ethan said.

Olivia couldn't help but laugh. "Unfailingly honest, aren't you?"

"Always," Ethan said. "But I'm a quick study."

Twila clapped her hands again. "Then it's a done deal? Two for the price of one?"

Olivia pulled in a deep breath and held it until it burned. When she let it out, she managed to nod. "That's fine with me. Really, it's up to Ethan, though. It's his time off from reality and putting up lights and hanging wreaths might qualify as too much reality."

"Well?" Heather said, bouncing on the tips of her toes with excitement. "What do you say?"

Ethan nodded. "Sure, why not? I'd be happy to help bring some magic to Holly Wreath."

CHAPTER 5

"Can you hand me that pry bar?" Olivia asked, pointing to her toolbox. "And the hammer?"

She was on her knees, looking at him over her shoulder with her vivid blue eyes and holding her hand out expectantly.

Ethan looked over the assortment of tools in her heavy metal box she stored them in. Finding it, he dug it out and said, "Here it is."

He put the tool into her outstretched hand, but she handed it back. "This is a crowbar."

Ethan bristled, his pride not wanting to admit not only that he'd never run a power tool, but that he couldn't even identify most of the tools she had in her box.

"Sorry. What's the difference?" he asked, laying it back where he'd found it.

"The pry bar is flat, so I can get these baseboards off without damaging them. It'd be a shame to break them when all they need is a little elbow grease to get them to shine again."

Ethan located the pry bar. "It seems like a lot of trouble to go through to salvage baseboards. It would have to be easier to get new ones."

"Obviously," Olivia said, carefully wedging the pry bar behind the baseboard and hammering it in deeper and carefully maneuvering it to loosen the wood. "Other than the exorbitant cost of buying all-new baseboard and trim for this gigantic house, I think reusing what's already here is a nice touch. They tell the story of this house. Of what it used to be. With a little sanding and a new coat of stain and polyurethane, you'd never suspect they weren't straight from the home improvement store. That's what I've done in every other room of this house. Or didn't you notice?"

The nails creaked as they were pulled from the wall. Once free, Olivia carefully laid the twelve-foot piece of wood on a pair of well-used sawhorses, and tapped out the nails, tossing them into a nearby waste basket.

"Right," Ethan said. "I didn't take a second look at the ones in my room, I guess."

Ethan stuck his hands into the front pockets of his jeans, mentally kicking himself for being such an idiot. It wasn't bad enough that he was basically useless after promising Twila he'd help Olivia, but he certainly didn't earn himself any bonus points by insulting her decision to be frugal.

Ethan looked around the room. It was spacious and had great light from three big windows that faced the south, but the room was one in the house that hadn't been updated yet. She'd redone the door that faced out in the hallway, and with it shut, Ethan would have never suspected she was in the middle of fixing it up.

"How come you haven't started on this room until now?" Ethan asked. Olivia eyed him, a clear frustration brewing beneath the surface, and he immediately regretted asking. Backpedaling, he tried to smooth things over. "What I mean is, you obviously know what you're doing. Take my bedroom for example. You did all that? It's amazing."

"Thanks," Olivia said cautiously. Moving over to the next baseboard, she tore it off and scribbled a number on the back of it to keep track of where it belonged when she was ready to rehang it.

"It's just, most places that open as a bed and breakfast would've done all the renovations beforehand, rather than trying to do them while operating with guests."

Olivia stood up and looked him in the eye. "Is this some kind of roundabout way of telling me you'd like a refund? Because I'd be happy to give it to you. I still have your cash on hand if you'd like it back."

"No, no. Sorry," Ethan raked a hand through his hair and huffed out a breath in exasperation. "This is coming out all wrong. I'm happy to be staying here, to get a break. I'm curious about you is all. What's your backstory? How'd you get into this kind of business?"

Olivia studied him for a beat before she dropped her eyes, focusing on the rusty nails she was tapping out.

"I'm sorry. I suppose I'm a bit sensitive to any perceived criticism about the house." She knocked the last nail out and set the baseboard on her growing pile. "This home feels like an extension of myself, if that makes sense. If it's not put together, then it seems like people are going to notice my life isn't put together, either."

Ethan nodded. "I can understand that."

Olivia smiled faintly. "I moved here to Holly Wreath almost ten years ago with my husband. We were newlyweds, and life felt like this grand adventure. He'd always wanted to open up a bed and breakfast and really sold me on the idea of having a big, spacious house where we could invite people in and let them slow down for a bit."

"You obviously found a place," Ethan said, hoping she didn't feel like she was being pressed.

"Yeah." Her gaze wandered around the room. "The only problem was, we were *poor* newlyweds, so we had to start from the bottom and build our way up. My grandfather had left me money for college but instead of going, I used it as a down payment on this place, with a few thousand dollars held back to restore it."

"What were you going to study in college?"

A look of genuine happiness crossed over Olivia's face, while she reminisced briefly, then slipped away altogether. "Music. Violin performance, actually."

"Ah. That makes sense. I could have sworn I heard violin music in my dreams last night. Were you practicing?"

Olivia's spine straightened, and she regarded him with wide eyes. "You heard that?"

"Yeah. Faintly."

"Sorry. I thought I was being careful keeping the doors shut and waiting until everyone was asleep."

"I didn't mind. From what I remember hearing while I was between sleep cycles, you're very talented."

Olivia turned her back and worked on the baseboard behind the door. "Yeah, well. I gave it up for a man who couldn't even stick with his own supposed lifelong dream long enough to see it finished."

Ethan shifted on his feet. He wanted to hear her story if she was willing to tell it. "He changed his mind?"

"The mounting debt and never-ending work on the house that wasn't going to bring in any money until we could get guests here started getting to him. I think he watched too many home repair shows and thought it'd be easy money but became disillusioned when he realized it wasn't. Jeff was always kind of attached to money. He wanted to have it, thinking it would make him happy, but we spent so long *not* as well off as he envisioned that it became the source of constant arguing. One day, he just left."

None of Olivia's confession was shocking. It hadn't been difficult for Ethan to guess that she was a single mom since he hadn't spotted any pictures of Olivia and Heather with a man in them. Olivia was clearly running the show all by herself, but as capable as she was, she looked tired for a woman who barely looked old enough to have a seven-year-old daughter.

"I'm sorry to hear that," Ethan said, feeling his own blood pressure rise, thinking that even though Mallory's reasons were different, she'd pulled something very similar when things weren't as rosy as she wanted them to be.

"After what he did to me and to Heather, I kind of resent money. I hate that we have to have it, I hate that everyone aspires to being rich, I hate that money and the pursuit of it takes the place of what matters most."

Ethan swallowed, wondering what Olivia would think of him if she knew how much money he had to his name. "It is unfortunate."

"In a perfect world, I would've had this entire house repainted and refinished before anyone ever stepped foot in it, but I needed to start making money, especially when my ex, Jeff, left. This is the last of the guest bedrooms that needs to be done, then I'll need to do some repairs outside, to our bedrooms, and on the living room. I don't doubt you missed the crack in the plaster by the chandelier."

"I...well..."

Olivia chuckled. "It's alright. I figured a guy like you doesn't miss anything. I did some quick painting to give the front rooms a facelift but they're going to need more than that. But first and foremost, the guests needed their rooms to be in good condition. People love staying in historic homes, but they won't stand for plaster sprinkling down on them while they sleep."

"No, I don't suppose." Olivia pried off another section of baseboard but before she could tamp out the nails, Ethan stepped between her and the sawhorses and took the piece from her. "Let me help."

"You think you can?"

Ethan chuckled, and he didn't miss how her eyes dropped down to his lips. "I watched you enough that I think I get the gist of what needs to be done."

Handing over the wood, Olivia said, "Go for it."

Ethan grabbed a hammer and asked, gesturing to the rest of the tools, "Where'd you learn to do all this stuff?"

"Home renovation?" Olivia asked. "Jeff was pretty good at it, so I learned a lot from being his unofficial apprentice. I learned a lot from my dad, too."

"Yeah? Does he come out and help once in a while?"

"He used to," Olivia said with a heavy sigh. "Both my parents are also gone. It's just me, Heather, and Twila now."

"I'm sorry to hear," Ethan said.

"Thanks. I was kind of their surprise miracle child when they were both already forty, so I'm glad I had them as long as I did."

Ethan twirled the hammer in his hand to get a feel for it. "So you've been on your own for a while now?"

"Pretty much. After Jeff was out of the picture, several well-meaning townspeople have traded an afternoon helping me put in windows or do plumbing in exchange for a home-cooked meal. The rest? YouTube."

"Seriously?" Ethan asked, pinching a nail and holding up the hammer, ready to strike.

Olivia shrugged. "Sure. Ninety percent of doing home improvements is having the gumption to try."

Ethan laughed. "Gumption? That sounds like some southern roots coming out."

"My granddaddy, actually. He was a proud South Carolinian. It about killed him that I was raised in the Yankee states just out of reach of the south."

Ethan shook his head, still grinning to himself, surprised at how much he was enjoying the late morning spent with Olivia. As he was fleeing Seattle, he had planned on moping around wherever he landed before getting back to work, throwing himself into his job to avoid thinking about Mallory. He hadn't planned on enjoying himself through service. She was letting her guard down, and when he was able to talk to her without sticking his foot in his mouth, he had an inkling that she might not dislike him as much as she surely had when they initially met.

He lined up his hammer, mentally coaching himself. "Here goes nothing."

Swinging hard, he crushed his thumb under the hammer, sending the board flying and himself reeling. Blinding white spots in his vision gave way to a painful throb in his thumb.

Olivia didn't hesitate and rushed to his side, taking his hand in hers so she could assess the damage.

"Are you alright?" she asked, rotating his thumb side to side.

"Everything but my pride." Ethan tried to laugh, but it came out as a pathetic groan. "That's the most painful thing I've experienced in a long while."

"I'm sure," Olivia said. "I've smashed my fingers a time or two, and sometimes, I think cutting my finger off would hurt less."

As the pain reduced to a dull ache, Ethan was acutely aware of the way Olivia's hands felt around his. They were petite and feminine but coarse from the hard work she was accustomed to. His face heated, and it had nothing to do with the extraordinary amount of pain he was in.

Olivia seemed to pick up on the change of mood in the room, and her breath hitched in her throat. Dropping his hand like it was a hot coal, she brushed a lock of hair behind her ear.

"Let me get an ice pack."

She hightailed it out of the room, her tool belt flopping with each step. Taking the moment alone to regroup, Ethan wanted to punch the wall. "That definitely didn't improve your image, idiot."

He paced the room, shaking his hand and trying to keep his mind off the discomfort of his bruised ego until Olivia returned.

Handing over the bag of ice she'd bundled in a kitchen towel, she said, "You really don't have much experience swinging a hammer, do you?"

"First time for everything, right?"

Olivia's mouth went agape. "You're kidding. Your bonafide first time using a hammer?"

Ethan snorted a laugh. "Bonafide?"

Rolling her eyes, she playfully shoved him. "You know what I mean."

"Yes, ma'am," Ethan drawled. "That was my first time using a hammer."

He was embarrassed to admit it, but Ethan knew she was going to find out sooner or later how inept he was. There was never any need for him to do it himself when he could employ someone else to do it, so he'd never tried.

Folding her arms, she said, "What is it exactly that you do?"

Putting his thumb in his mouth and sucking on it to draw out the pain, Ethan gave himself a second to figure out how to answer. His escape from life was giving him a brief moment to enjoy anonymity, especially when it came to his money. He'd been to too many parties and social engagements where women fawned over him and men befriended him with the hope that they might get something from him. He wanted something different for once.

He leaned back against the wall and wrapped his finger in the cold towel. "You know. Corporate America and all."

"Your whole life? Like, your dad never helped you build a birdhouse or anything?"

Ethan shook his head and took his thumb out of his mouth, shaking his hand. "Nope. Parents died when I was four, remember?"

Olivia's face went pale, and she grabbed his forearm again. He tried to hold back a smile, but he was quickly discovering he didn't mind one bit when she touched him.

"I'm so sorry. I forgot. You told me they were coming home from a party. I didn't mean to—"

Ethan waved his hand in the air, dismissing her comment. "It was a long time ago. I barely remember them."

"Still, that had to be rough. It's hard to miss something you wish you had, too."

"Yeah," Ethan said softly. "I guess that's true."

"I can see why you don't love Christmas."

A vision of Mallory flashed in his mind. She knew he hated the Christmas season because it was a reminder that his parents had been taken from him too early, but still, she'd decided to leave him when he was most vulnerable. "That has a lot to do with it, I suppose. This December's been particularly rough, though."

"Well, I don't love Christmas as much as I used to, either. Jeff kind of ruined it for me."

Ethan strode over to the baseboard he'd sent flying through the air and picked up the hammer he'd dropped. "It'll be nice to have someone to commiserate with."

"Promise me one thing, though," Olivia said. Her face was pleading ,and Ethan knew she was being serious.

"As long as you don't ask me to use a saw, because I'm starting to think you're right, and I might end up cutting off my arm. Otherwise, you name it."

Olivia tilted her head back and peered up into his face, making Ethan swallow. Her flowery perfume was unassuming and faint but made his blood pump a little faster. "You can't even grumble under your breath when Heather is around. I know it's probably foolish to want to keep her naïve and innocent, but one of the last joys at this time of the year that I have is watching her enjoy Christmas."

Ethan nodded, pinched his fingers together, and pretended to zip his lips. "Not a word."

"Not even one cynical comment about Santa? She still believes in him."

"She does? I thought kids stopped believing in him when their friends ruined it for them in kindergarten."

Olivia swatted the back of her hand at his stomach. "Promise."

Ethan chortled while scooting away to defend himself. "I'm just kidding. I might be on Santa's naughty list, but I cross my heart I won't breathe a word of it to Heather."

"Good," Olivia said, retreating a step back. "As long as Heather can have the kind of Christmas every kid deserves, you and I can be Scrooges together."

CHAPTER 6

"This is really nice," Ethan said as he drove down main street. "I hadn't seen most of this when I came into town yesterday."

Olivia shifted in her seat and sat on her hands. She hadn't ridden alone in a man's car since the last time she'd been on a date, and that was at least two years earlier. The whole thing felt strangely personal. They were locked in a tiny space together, and they were close enough she could smell the clean scent of the button-up shirt he'd changed into when they were done pulling off baseboards and had gotten a good start on stripping off the wallpaper. She'd offered to take her own car, but Ethan had dismissed the idea, saying it didn't make sense to waste gas when they were going to the same place anyway.

"Holly Wreath does go all-out for Christmas. It's kind of our thing," Olivia said.

"I suppose it's ironic that you and I ended up in this town, isn't it? The two of us grumpy about Christmas in the middle of it all."

"A bit, yeah," Olivia said with a laugh.

Ethan gawked at the thirty-foot blue spruce that had been hauled to town square. "Do they do one of those tree lightings here?"

"Yeah. Next weekend, actually," Olivia said. "It's part of the festival and is a lot of fun. It's like the whole town comes out, everyone keeps warm by huddling under blankets and passing around hot chocolate—"

"Your hot chocolate, I hope?"

Warmth seeped through her cheeks, bringing with it the urge to giggle stupidly at his roundabout compliment. Olivia had to look out the window so he couldn't see her biting her lip.

"Nope," Olivia said. "It's the boxed packets dumped into hot water. I don't produce mine on a mass scale. It'd lose some of its charm, I think."

"That's too bad," Ethan said, winking at Olivia and making her blush rage anew. "I don't think I can ever go back to store bought after having yours. If you make me another mug of hot chocolate before I leave, I think I could die happy."

"What Holly Wreath Inn guests want, Holly Wreath Inn guests get."

"I'm holding you to that." Ethan smirked, and Olivia matched him with a smile of her own. "So, do they do a choir to sing Christmas carols?"

"Not officially. Usually, people start their own impromptu Christmas songs, but this year, the town council asked Twila to have a little more structure so yes, there's supposed to be a more formal musical presentation. The whole event is becoming a pretty big shindig for out-of-towners. Holly Wreath gets a lot of traffic that day, so they want it to be extra special to entice people to keep coming back."

"To spend their money," Ethan said.

"Bingo," Olivia said, snapping her fingers. "It's a boon to the economy around here, and people who run businesses around this area could definitely use it."

"And that's where we, the decoration committee, come in. To make Main Street look festive so people will break out in Christmas song."

Olivia raised an eyebrow and asked, "Can you resist singing along to a Christmas song while everyone else is happily doing it around you?"

Ethan drummed his fingers on the steering wheel and shrugged. "Can't remember the last time I had the opportunity. I suppose I'll have to stick around and see what all the fuss is about."

Olivia's gaze snapped over to Ethan. He was paying attention to traffic, giving Olivia a chance to admire his handsome profile. She had to wedge her hands further under her legs to keep from running her fingers along his jawline. He'd shaved, and she'd missed the feel of a man's cleanly shaven skin.

"You're thinking of staying longer in Holly Wreath? You only booked your room through next Friday."

"You have other guests who need the room?"

"No," Olivia said a little too quickly. "I mean, I don't have anyone else coming, but I assumed you had to get back to your job in Corporate America. From what I've always understood, the business world waits for no one."

"It'll be there when I get back," Ethan said. "Besides, a lot of it I can do remotely. That's the beauty of working where I do."

"That must be nice," Olivia said. "To come and go as you please."

"My sister is keeping watch over things while I'm gone, so I didn't totally abandon ship."

"You work with your sister?"

"Yeah," Ethan said, scratching his fingertips along his jawline. "We run a family business together. It's the legacy our parents left us."

"I see," Olivia said, trying to tamp down the excitement that was bubbling in her stomach. It wasn't just the thought that she had a paying customer for another day, but it was that Ethan was staying longer. She'd decided he wasn't nearly as grumpy and impersonal as she had pegged him to be when he was eating at the diner. "Well, in that case, you're in for a treat. The Christmas tree lighting is pure magic."

"Magic? I thought you weren't into Christmas."

"I don't hate it, per se. The season just holds a lot of painful memories. Even you have to admit there are elements of Christmas that stir something in the soul."

A crooked grin graced Ethan's lips, and he conceded, "Yeah. Some of it's alright. Not enough to make me a converted Scrooge though."

Olivia laughed loudly, hoping she didn't sound like a ditz. Spotting Twila out her window, she pointed her out to Ethan. "Twila's already waiting for us. There's a parking spot across the street, too. You might want to take it. It looks awfully busy down here today."

"Must be the Friday lunch crowd."

"No doubt. Friday was always one of our bigger days at the diner."

Ethan put on his signal and maneuvered into the spot, then killed the engine. He leaned over the steering wheel to get a better view of the shops in the historic Main Street buildings.

"I see Holly Wreath has some higher quality establishments than where I first met you."

Olivia's jaw dropped, and she punched him lightly on the arm, noticing his firm bicep under his coat. "I resent that. The diner is...quaint."

"Quaint, sure, but even you have to admit the food is cafeteria quality. Like, prison cafeteria."

Olivia's eyes rolled. "You're a food snob, aren't you?"

"If I'm going to use up those calories, I want to feel like I'm not wasting them."

"Oh, it's worse," Olivia said.

Ethan quirked his head. "What is?"

Olivia's lips twitched with an unexpressed smile. "You're a health nut. Counting calories and all."

"Now you're starting to sound like my sister."

Humor seeped through Olivia. "It sounds like your sister and I would get along famously."

"It certainly seems that way. Although if you keep feeding me hot chocolate and cinnamon rolls, I'm going to be waddling the next time I see her."

"So, no bread pudding with our stew for dinner tonight?"

Ethan's hazel eyes sparkled, and Olivia felt like she could get lost in them. "I'll just be sure to do a few extra sit ups before bed. If you're making it, I'm sure it'll be worth the cost."

Olivia stared too long, and so did Ethan. For a second, she couldn't think of anything to say, but the silence wasn't as uncomfortable as it had been that morning. A truck driver honked and leaned out the window to wave at Twila, snapping them out of it. They both chortled uncomfortably, and Olivia wondered if Ethan felt the same connection she did, or if it was all in her head.

Ethan undid his seatbelt and grabbed his door handle. "Hang on a second."

Before Olivia could ask why, Ethan was out of the car and had trotted around the front to open her door. Offering his hand to help her, she accepted and stepped out, holding the top of her coat closed to keep the chilly air from plunging down her neck. "How gentlemanly of you."

Ethan shut the door and made sure it was locked. "I suppose it's the product of being raised by your socially strict grandparents. I'm doomed to do everything the way their generation did it."

"No complaints about that here," Olivia said, keeping to herself that Jeff had never been big on chivalry. "Of course, don't be getting any ideas into your head that I'm one of those women that needs rescuing."

"I would never," Ethan said with a devilishly handsome grin.

He was still holding her hand as he led her to the back of the BMW, and they waited for a clearing in the traffic. When they had the chance, they dashed across the street to where Twila was waiting for them with an entertained sparkle in her eyes as she watched them over the rims of her glasses. When they made it to the curb, Ethan let go of Olivia's hand, making her heart sink a little. She chided herself for being ridiculous, but without his hand wrapped around hers, her skin felt cold, and not because of the weather. Taking in a refreshing breath of the crisp air, her spirit felt unencumbered by the worries that usually plagued her during the Christmas season, which was a welcome relief from the sadness that had threatened to crumble in on her the day before.

"Hello, Twila," Ethan said cordially. "It's a beautiful day out, isn't it?"

"It certainly is starting to feel a lot like Christmas." She narrowed her eyes at him and cocked her head.

Ethan's eyes shifted back and forth. "What?"

"Are you *sure* we've never met before? I keep getting this feeling of déjà vu every time I see you."

Ethan chuckled. "Like I said before, I'm sure I would have remembered meeting a lady like you."

"Twila is hard to forget," Olivia agreed.

Still trying to put her finger on the mystery, Twila asked, "What'd you say your last name was?"

"I didn't."

Twila scoffed and threw her hands up in good-natured exasperation. "Are you going to tell me or do I have to ask the sheriff for a favor and have him pull you over in your fancy car so he can see your driver's license?"

Ethan's delight twinkled in his gorgeous eyes, and he looked like a small boy who'd managed to steal a treat from the cookie jar without getting caught. "That won't be necessary. My last name's Wilder."

"Ethan Wilder," Twila said, mulling over his name while Ethan watched her with keen interest.

Twila shrugged. "Huh. I thought it was ringing a bell, but my old brain can't seem to figure out which bell it was."

"I really do have one of those faces, I think," Ethan said.

"I suppose," Twila agreed.

"If it makes you feel any better, I get the same feeling," Olivia said. "He definitely looks like the kind of guy people would know about."

Ethan's jaw tightened, and if Olivia wasn't reading him wrong, he squirmed uncomfortably. "That depends on who you're talking to. To most, I'm your average nobody."

Twila patted his arm, appearing very amused by his attempt at self-deprecation. "I highly doubt that. You belong on the cover of a magazine if you ask me."

Ethan produced a lopsided grin as he dropped his head and rubbed the back of his neck.

"So," Olivia said to take Twila's attention off of Ethan, "what do you need help with today?"

"I'm putting up the rest of the Main Street decorations. One more block worth of these little light strands and candy cane striped ribbon wrapped around the light posts and we'll be set," Twila said, nudging a tote of decorations with the toe of her boot. "Can one of you crawl up the ladder for me? I'll sort out the lights and ribbon, and the other person can hand the stuff up the ladder."

"I can do it," Ethan said, moving to take the ladder to the first lamp.

"Hold on there," Olivia said, snagging him by the hem of his coat. "I saw what you did with the hammer this morning, and I'm not so sure you should be scaling ladders. Have you ever even climbed one? You might end up with a broken neck with your track record."

"I've climbed plenty of ladders," Ethan said.

Olivia crossed her arms and cocked an eyebrow. "Really? Because I wouldn't be surprised one bit if you were lying to save face."

"My sister and I had a treehouse," Ethan said, proudly jutting his chin out in response.

"So, you haven't been on a ladder in what, twenty years?" Olivia challenged.

Ethan challenged Olivia by stepping closer. "It's only been about fifteen."

Unwilling to back down, she closed the gap and was toe to toe with him. "Ha! Well, I practically live on a ladder. You can spot me so you don't take a tumble and knock yourself out. We can't have the mysterious stranger who's breezed into town with a case of amnesia. Corporate America would miss you."

"You have no idea," Ethan muttered as Olivia took the first step up the ladder.

"Huh?"

"Never mind." Ethan shook his head. "Besides, my sister would be able to find me if I was lost in the middle of the Amazon rainforest and I was *trying* to hide from her."

Olivia made it to the top of the ladder and reached back for the rolls of red and white ribbon Twila was holding. Twila asked, "Oh, yeah? Sister a bit clingy? I have one like that. Calls me every weekend to make sure I haven't gotten myself into any trouble."

"Clingy? Nah. Nosy is more like it." Ethan put his foot on the bottom rung of the ladder and held either side to keep it steady. "It comes with the territory when you're a twin."

"She's your twin?" Olivia asked. "I always wondered what that would be like."

"For starters, it's not as fun as you're thinking. We still bickered like any siblings would do, and in reality, it's probably worse than most. We've been in competition ever since we came out of the womb."

Olivia secured the red ribbon, twisting it around and around, then handing it to Twila when she could reach it. "I was an only child, so I can't comment on sibling rivalry."

"For one, she's always beating me at everything. She was born first, finished college with a higher GPA, got married first."

"Surely you have girls lined up down the block to have you walk them down the aisle," Twila said.

"Twila," Olivia moaned. "I'm sure he doesn't want to discuss his dating life with a couple of women he barely knows."

"What should we talk about then?" Twila asked. She was playing innocent, but Olivia knew her well enough that nothing she ever did was without an end goal in mind.

"How about the tree lighting ceremony? Is everything all set for it? Have you bought up Holly Wreath's supply of hot chocolate?"

"Just about," Twila said. "I had to call over to the next town's grocery stores to find enough cups. Are you going to be sticking around, Ethan? It's the highlight of the year."

"As a matter of fact, I am. Olivia convinced me that I couldn't miss the magic."

"She did, did she?" Twila said. "Then maybe you can help me convince her to do something I've been begging her to do for almost the past decade."

"What's that?" Ethan asked, holding up a hand to shield it from the sun as he gazed up at Olivia. Olivia pretended she didn't notice that they were talking about her and kept fussing with the ribbon to make sure it was laying just right. Wrinkles wouldn't do at the Holly Wreath Christmas Festival.

"She has an amazing gift with the violin," Twila said.

"So I've heard," Ethan said.

Twila about dropped the strand of lights she was holding. "She played for you?"

"Unintentionally," Olivia interjected. "I thought he was asleep and that he wouldn't be able to hear me on the other side of the house."

"Ah. I was going to express my surprise," Twila said. "In all the years living here, I've only convinced her to play for me on a handful of occasions. I think she'd more readily agree to having her teeth pulled."

"And why do you suppose that is?" Ethan asked.

Twila and Ethan both looked up at Olivia. She snapped and pointed at the lights Twila still hadn't picked up. "You already know the answer, Twila."

"But why? You're hiding your talent under a bushel, and that's a crying shame as far as I'm concerned. You're robbing the world of hearing your gift. It's not right."

Ethan picked up the lights and handed them to Olivia, who began winding them around the lamp post. "Where are you wanting Olivia to play?"

"At the tree lighting. The town council's been on me to

ramp up the whole festival weekend since it's really started taking off. People visiting from all over, coming from out of state even. Having her serenade the crowd with a beautiful Christmas hymn or two would be the cherry on top. Don't you think, Olivia?"

Olivia's words were clipped as she answered Twila's pleading. "Why can't you accept that I'm not good enough to play in front of hundreds of people?"

"Because that's the most ridiculous thing I've ever heard you say. I know how talented you are," Twila said, with a hunger in her eye that Olivia knew wouldn't be satiated until she agreed.

"I don't have time to practice. Sure, I can play a couple of songs decently, but one of the worst sounds in the world is listening to a screeching violin. That would be an automatic killjoy to the tree lighting."

Ethan's lips were pressed together, and he nodded, thoughtfully listening to Olivia's concerns. When she finished, he rubbed his hands together, then pressed them against his chin. "I tell you what. I think I might be able to help you."

"Help me? How? Do *you* happen to play the violin, and you're volunteering to take my place?"

"Not exactly," Ethan said with a chuckle, "but I can give you the gift of time. So you can practice and be ready for the show."

"Time?" Olivia repeated the word like it was completely foreign to her.

"Yeah. I'll cook some of the meals, do the dishes..." Ethan scratched his head as he thought. "I might not be much use with tools, but I can peel off wallpaper, and I'm sure there are a dozen other menial tasks you could teach me to do."

"That feels wrong," Olivia said, shaking her head.

"Why? Because you're too stubborn to ask people for help?" Twila challenged.

"No," Olivia shot back. "He's a paying customer. I'm not running a dude ranch where he pays me to do the chores."

"Maybe you should look into that as a business model," Ethan said with a smirk. "It could work. It apparently does for a lot of ranchers."

Twila and Ethan laughed while Olivia leaned against the top of the ladder, and looked the opposite way down the sidewalk, watching people come and go, wishing she could escape the entrapment she was facing.

"I'm being serious," Olivia said.

Ethan's eyes locked on hers, and she was powerless to look away. "So am I. I appreciate you wanting me to have a relaxing vacation, but I think a bit of community service is exactly what I need. You know. Get me in the Christmas spirit and all."

Olivia wanted to protest, but she couldn't find the words. "I don't think this is going to be a good idea."

"So, you'll do it?" Twila clasped her hands together, ready to cheer if Olivia accepted.

"Fine. But if I freeze up or fail miserably, I'm tossing your luggage out in the snow," she pointed at Ethan, then to Twila, "and I don't think I'll be inviting you over for any more Sunday dinners."

Ethan's smile was intoxicatingly handsome, and that in itself was an amazing reward for Olivia's bravery.

"I'll wager that you'll do splendidly. I'm so pleased!" Twila squealed, causing a few people to turn and look, only to realize it was just Twila being herself. Bending over and rummaging through a large purse she had set on top of one of her holiday décor totes, she pulled out a stack of paper and handed it up to Olivia.

Olivia scrunched up her nose. "What's this?"

"The music. I've been carrying it around the past couple of weeks, hoping I'd find a way to get you to agree. I owe you big time, Ethan. I had no idea how I was going to do it, but you made it all too easy."

"I can hardly wait to hear Olivia perform. If it's half as good as I suspect, she's much more talented than she cares to admit."

Olivia sifted through the sheets of music, her eyes running over the notes but only seeing them as blurs of black and white. Her pulse pounded in her temples. Twila had had the foresight to choose something simple that Olivia would have no trouble playing when she practiced. It was the anxious thought of playing in front of all the tourists and towns folks that raised her blood pressure.

"Now, back to you, Ethan Wilder. Tell me about yourself. Do you have a girlfriend?"

Olivia could feel herself leaning down to hear his answer. The voice in the back of her head told her it didn't matter what his answer was, but she wanted to know all the same. While pretending she was still engrossed in the music, she didn't see a flock of pigeons that flew out of the courthouse steeple, and in their scattered flight, headed right for Olivia.

The birds sped past, startled that they hadn't noticed Olivia until they were on a collision course. Feeling herself tipping off the ladder, she was unable to stop herself. A shrill scream escaped her as she tumbled.

Bracing herself to hit the unforgiving concrete, she pinched her eyes shut. A pair of strong arms caught her midair.

"I've got you," Ethan said, holding her close to him.

When her pulse calmed down, and she opened her eyes, the concern she saw in Ethan's face made her heart rate rev all over again.

"You caught me," Olivia said, still astonished that she was

in his arms and not flat on her back, shattered into a thousand pieces on the sidewalk.

"I did," Ethan said, with a smile that showcased his perfect teeth. "I know you said you didn't need rescuing, but maybe you do."

CHAPTER 7

"The spices are all in that drawer," Heather said, pointing to a set of cabinets to the right of the sink.

"This one?" Ethan asked, opening it when Heather nodded. Sifting through the dozens of jars, he found the paprika. "Here we go."

Heather scrunched up her nose. "Are you sure this is going to be good? I only like salt and pepper in my scrambled eggs, and sometimes, not at all."

"Step aside, young lady, and see what you've been missing all your life," Ethan said. He sprinkled a dash of paprika into the bowl and whisked it into the eggs. He'd heated up a frying pan on the stove, and when he poured the beaten eggs in it, they sizzled and bubbled deliciously.

"I guess we can always feed her cereal if it doesn't taste good," Heather said.

"Oh, ye of little faith," Ethan said as he stirred the eggs. "One of the cooks I had growing up was from Mexico, and she'd make the best smoky, spicy eggs anyone's ever had."

Heather tipped her head and looked at him with puzzlement. "You had a cook growing up?"

"Yeah, I did. She worked for my grandparents who raised me after my parents died."

"So, are you rich?" Heather jumped up onto the counter next to the stove, swinging her legs and leaning over to see what he was doing.

"I'm well enough off." Ethan spread out the plates Heather had gotten for him and put a warm homemade tortilla on all three of them.

"That sounds like something a rich guy would say so he didn't sound like he had a ton of money," Heather said.

Ethan couldn't help but laugh at her perceptiveness. So far, he'd been able to keep a low profile in Holly Wreath—no one had commented that they'd recognized him, and he hadn't seen himself on any magazines when he ran errands for Olivia—and he was enjoying it immensely. It was nice not to have to keep up appearances for anyone like he did in Seattle. He certainly didn't need anyone offering their condolences when they found out his engagement with Mallory was off. It'd been a high profile match, and he was surprised the media hadn't had more of a frenzy with it. Then it would only be a matter of time before unflattering pictures of him were plastered all over the tabloids

"Is the juice ready?" Ethan asked as he laid the eggs in the middle of each tortilla.

"It's in the fridge." Heather jumped off and raced across the kitchen like she was afraid Ethan might get to it first.

Ethan glanced at the clock on the stove. It was already almost eight, and he was surprised Olivia hadn't woken up when he had snuck into the kitchen at seven to make her breakfast. She'd been a ball of nerves all week practicing for the tree lighting, and though she tried to hide it, he kept finding her with a faraway look in her eyes, and when she snapped out of it and came back to the real world, she was always apologetic and embarrassed. In an attempt to ease the pressure she felt, he'd offered to be her audience so she could get used to playing in front of people.

"Playing for one person is worse than playing for an entire crowd," Olivia had said while she had taken a break from practicing, and they were repairing some spots of plaster in the guest bedroom. "In a sea of people, I don't have to look at anyone in particular but one on one, I'll be able to see the disapproval in their eyes on a very personal level."

"And why are you assuming anyone'll disapprove?" Ethan had asked.

Her shoulders had risen and fallen in a weak shrug. "I was fresh out of high school the last time I performed in front of anyone, and in case you've forgotten, I never went to college. Any skills I had are rustier than my car, so I'm thinking it was a bit pretentious of me to think I could ever be a performing soloist in the first place. The thing that used to thrill me is now terrifying because I'm not sure I'm good enough. In fact, I'm positive I'm not."

"Yes, you are."

Olivia had scoffed. "Even you've only heard me through closed doors."

"And closed doors don't generally make anything sound better," Ethan had answered with folded arms. "I'll tell you what. I'll give you the rest of the week to practice, but you have to agree to play for me the morning of the tree lighting ceremony. If it really is scarier to play for one person, you'll get it out of you, and it'll be less frightening that evening in front of a crowd, right?"

Olivia had scrunched her lips and moved them off to the side, and Ethan could still remember how adorable she'd looked while she considered his offer. She had had a splatter of drywall spackling on her cheek, and it had taken all his self-control not to reach over to her face and wipe it off.

"Alright," she'd finally said. "As long as you give me a few more days to mentally prepare."

"Deal," Ethan had agreed.

"Earth to Ethan," he heard Heather's voice bringing him back into the present. "It's a little early to be daydreaming, isn't it?"

Ethan laughed as he rolled up the burritos and set them on the table. He'd swung by the florist the night before and bought a bouquet that he hoped Olivia would like. He had no idea what her favorite flower was—he hardly knew anything about her. All he was sure of was that he wanted to know everything.

"You sound like my grandpa," Ethan said, setting out a bowl of fresh cut fruit. "He always thought I had my head in the clouds. I think that's been the key to my success, though. Thinking outside the box."

"I'll see if that works on my mom," Heather said as she picked a grape out of the bowl of fruit. "Daydreaming gets me in trouble for not taking out the trash. The funny thing is, my mom spaces out worse than I do."

Ethan grinned as he folded napkins and put them under the silverware. He was going to ask her if she happened to know what her mom's favorite flower was but their conversation was interrupted by the ring of the doorbell. Heather looked at Ethan, and he shrugged. It wasn't his place to be answering doors. As comfortable as he'd made himself at the inn, he was still technically a guest.

"I'll get it," Heather said, sliding off her seat and skipping to the door.

Ethan found the dish soap and filled up the sink so he could tidy the kitchen, hoping Olivia would wake up soon. Today was the day she'd agreed to play through her songs for him, and he was looking forward to it.

"There's a pretty lady at the door, and she said she's

looking for you," Heather said as she moseyed back into the kitchen.

"A pretty lady?" Ethan repeated. "Did she tell you her name?"

"No. Should I go ask?" Heather poked her thumb behind her. "I told her I'd go get you, so if you didn't want me to tell her that, you'll have to sneak out the back door, then I can tell her you went to the gym or something. That's what Twila tells my mom to do when she doesn't want to talk to somebody."

If it was Mallory, he might've taken Heather up on her offer.

"No, I'll go see who it is," Ethan said. As he patted his hands dry on the dish towel, Olivia came rushing into the kitchen.

Raking her hands through her hair to try and smooth it into a ponytail, her eyes were glossed over with panic. "Was that the doorbell?"

"Relax, Mom. I got it," Heather said from where she was perched back atop her chair. "Besides, it's for Ethan."

Olivia's blue eyes moved back to him. "Are you expecting someone?"

"Nope," Ethan said, keeping his voice low and praying his ex hadn't somehow managed to track him down.

Worse than her groveling for him to take her back, would be her groveling while Olivia watched. Yes, what Mallory had done was inexcusable, but he was over it. Every passing day distanced him from their relationship, and the more he thought about it, the more obvious it was that they were all wrong for each other from the start.

Olivia stepped closer and whispered, "Do you want to sneak out the back? I can cover for you."

Ethan couldn't help a laugh from coming out. "Heather

already told me about that little tactic you use. You'll never be able to use it on me, now."

"What makes you think I don't have other tricks to evade people?" Olivia teased.

Ethan laughed again at her. "Thanks, but nah, I've got it. I can't imagine who'd be looking for me here. Only Peg, my secretary knows where I am. Please. Help yourself to breakfast. Heather helped me put it together."

"If you don't like it, it's all on him, though," Heather said. "I told him not to add paprika."

Ethan headed for the front door. Heather hadn't invited the woman inside, and the door was closed to keep the cold morning air out. Even through the muted glass window, Ethan could tell who it was shivering on the front step.

Ethan swung open the door. "Emma?"

Emma didn't wait to be invited in and shoved her way through to the entryway. "Took you long enough. I'm pretty sure the tips of my fingers are dead from frostbite."

"What are you doing here? How'd you find me?"

Emma unwrapped the scarf around her neck and smirked at her brother. "It was hardly difficult. I brought a box of chocolates into the office to share and Peg sang like a canary."

Ethan moaned and covered his eyes with his hand. "I thought she had tighter lips than that. Chocolate was all it took to do her in?"

"I found out hazelnut crèmes are her favorite." Emma shrugged off her coat. "Besides, she always did like me better. Can you blame her?"

Emma let herself into the front sitting room, turning a full circle to take in the space while Ethan wondered what he was supposed to do with his sister. He liked where things were going with Olivia, though they were still in precarious territory. One blabbing comment from Emma might undo all the careful and calculated flirting. He was sure Olivia had budding feelings for him, too, and though she kept her heart guarded, he had caught glimpses when she wasn't being so cautious.

"Why'd you come?" Ethan said. "It's one thing to find out where I've been hiding out. This is a little more than a trip across town to see how I'm doing."

"You're telling me," Emma said. "I was surprised you picked something so remote. Our pilot had to practically land the business jet in the middle of a cornfield that they call the airport. And this weather! I'm going to have to take a trip to Hawaii to recuperate."

"It's not so bad. Makes sitting by a woodburning stove downright cozy," Ethan said right as Olivia walked in.

Emma's eyebrows shot up when she saw Olivia. Looking squarely at her brother, Emma said, "I'm sure snuggling up by the fire is very cozy."

Ethan rolled his eyes at his sister's insinuation that he hadn't missed. The thought made Ethan's mind wander, and he let himself admit that snuggling with Olivia on the couch in front of a fire would make the cold that had settled in Holly Wreath exponentially more enjoyable.

Olivia had tamed her hair and was the appearance of poise, even though Ethan knew she'd been scrambling only moments before. Graciously, Olivia extended her hand to Emma.

"Hello, I'm Olivia Campbell, the owner of Holly Wreath Inn."

"Emma Bryant," she said, giving Olivia the kind of firm handshake Emma had perfected over the years working in business. "Ethan here tells me he's having a wonderful time. I for one can say I've never seen him so relaxed."

"Is that so?" Olivia asked, clasping her hands and sneaking a quick peek at Ethan.

Emma pointed to his neck. "He's undone the top button of his shirt. That might as well be a sign from Heaven. I can't remember the last time I saw him without a tie when he's not at the gym."

Ethan noticed there was a question in Olivia's eyes as she held her smile. "You know Ethan very well, then?"

Ethan stepped over to his sister and draped his arm around Emma's shoulders, tugging her close in an obnoxious way that he knew Emma hated. "Emma's my sister. The one I was telling you about?"

"Ah. Right," Olivia said, looking relieved. "I can see the resemblance now."

"We both have the same color of eyes as our mom, our hair color from our dad, but I maintain I got the cuter nose," Emma said.

"I told you I couldn't get away from her," Ethan said. Emma elbowed him in the ribs.

Olivia gestured to the armchair and offered, "Why don't I let you two catch up? I can bring you something out here if you'd like. Some hot apple cider?"

"Actually, I made enough breakfast that she can join us in the kitchen," Ethan said. "Unless you'd rather eat in the dining room."

"You? Made breakfast?" The smirk on Emma's face told him she was going to grill him the first chance she got.

"Olivia has a big day ahead of her, and I thought I'd help out," Ethan said, hoping he sounded nonchalant. "It's just the eggs and salsa Lucinda likes to make."

Emma's eyes shifted between Olivia and Ethan, and he wished he could pin down what she was thinking. "I'd love to have breakfast with you."

"Right in here," Olivia said, leading the way back to the kitchen where Heather was sitting on her fidgety hands.

"Took you long enough," Heather said. "I'm so starving that Ethan's eggs are starting to smell good."

Olivia pursed her lips at Heather, then gave an apologetic look to Ethan.

"I'll bet you'll be licking your plate by the time we're done," Ethan said to Heather with an amused smirk.

Olivia got out another plate, handing it to Ethan. He spread eggs on a tortilla for Emma and wrapped it tightly. She thanked him and sat down between Heather and Olivia, while Olivia's blue eyes still soaked in everything. Ethan had learned she had an eye for detail and wasn't going to miss a thing, a trait he also prided himself on.

Olivia asked Heather to say grace, and she offered a quick prayer of thanks. Picking up his fork, Ethan helped himself to a generous portion of fruit, then passed it to Olivia. Her fingers brushed across his, and he was sure her cheeks grew pinker. Emma noticed, too. Swallowing the strawberry he was chewing, he said to his sister, "I'm assuming you're headed back since you found where I am and now your worries are put to rest?"

"Nope," Emma said, blowing into the hot burrito. "I have the whole weekend off, and I thought I'd hang out with my baby brother since I haven't seen you in a month."

"Without Rob? Isn't he going to miss you?" Ethan said. A gnawing worry that his sister was up to something had imbedded itself into his brain.

"Of course he misses me. We're newlyweds and still very much in the honeymoon phase," Emma said with a twinkle in her eye. "But he's doing some boring doctor training, so he's tied up the whole weekend."

"When was the wedding?" Olivia asked.

"Last month," Emma said, adjusting the giant wedding ring on her finger. "Just got back from our honeymoon to Cabo."

"Cabo? Wow. I bet it was beautiful," Olivia said.

"Where's that?" Heather asked. Ethan noticed she'd chowed down on her burrito and was only a bite away from finishing.

"It's in Mexico," Ethan said.

"Oh," Heather said, stuffing the last of her food into her mouth. "I like your ring."

"This?" Emma said, holding up her hand and wriggling her fingers to admire the shine. "Me, too. I think Rob did a superb job picking it. It's very me."

Ethan rolled his eyes, hoping Olivia didn't think Emma was rubbing in just how expensive a piece of jewelry like that could be. Emma had always been drawn to shiny things, not because of the cost, but because of how they sparkled. Of course, she'd never wanted for anything, so it was easy for Emma to pick and choose when money was no object.

"Congratulations on your marriage," Olivia said without a hint of cynicism. "Er, best of luck. I can't remember which one my mom told me I'm supposed to say to the bride."

"It's all good. I for one can't remember being so happy," Emma gushed. "I didn't think marriage would suit me, being as stubborn and independent as I am, but it really does."

"Stubborn and independent is an understatement," Ethan teased under his breath, earning him another swat from his sister.

Olivia wiped her mouth with her napkin and said, "I'm very happy for you."

"Thanks. Now I just need to find the right girl for Ethan," Emma said, tapping her fingernail on the table in his direction.

Ethan coughed, choking on his eggs. In a warning tone, he said, "Emma..."

"What? I can't want the same happiness for my brother as I have for myself?"

"Anyway," Ethan said, changing the subject to something that didn't make him want to squirm in his seat, hoping Emma didn't bring up Mallory in conversation, "where are you planning on staying since you insist on following me around Holly Wreath?"

"Actually," Emma said, setting her hands down on the table, "I'm looking for a room. Do you have anything available Olivia?"

"Yes, I do," Olivia said at the same time Ethan said no.

"You came all the way here without a place to stay? What if everything was booked?" Ethan asked.

Emma shrugged, unconcerned that she might have been homeless for the weekend. "If nothing else, I would've found you, and you, being the good brother than you are, would've offered me your room."

Ethan sat back in his chair and crossed his arms across his stomach. "And where would I have slept?"

"On the couch," Emma said. "Obviously."

Olivia laughed. "There's no need to displace anyone. I've got two more bedrooms upstairs available. I'll just need an hour to get everything ready."

"Oh, no rush. I'll be spending the day with Ethan. I want to take a look around this charming town. Everything's so... Christmas-y."

"You haven't seen anything yet," Heather said, perking up. "Tonight's the tree lighting. You can come with us."

"Ooo, a tree lighting? I'd love to!" Emma said.

"So you like Christmas?" Olivia asked, her eyes turning to Ethan and a new smile twitching at the corner of her lips.

Emma finished off her glass of orange juice. "Why wouldn't I? It's the best time of the year."

"I got a different impression about your family's views on Christmas from Ethan," Olivia said.

Emma wafted her hand in the air. "Ethan? He's a regular

Grinch, which is another reason I'm surprised he's hung around here. Usually he hightails it whenever anyone even so much as mentions Santa or stockings. Is the tree lighting a big deal?"

"One of the biggest deals of the whole year," Heather bragged.

"Speaking of the tree lighting," Ethan said, turning his attention to Olivia, "you promised to practice performing your violin pieces for me today."

Olivia's smile evaporated, and she looked irked enough to toss him and his suitcase out in the snow.

"As much as I'd love to, I actually have to get Heather to school," Olivia said, scooting out from her seat and piling her dishes onto her empty plate.

"I don't have to go for another ten minutes," Heather said, spearing the last blueberry on her plate.

"Then maybe we'll actually get you there on time today," Olivia said.

"It's alright. We'll wait here," Emma said. Patting Ethan on the forearm, she looked him in the eye. "Turns out, Ethan and I do have some catching up to do. We can wait to explore Holly Wreath until later."

Olivia's countenance fell as she realized she wasn't going to get out of it. "Alright. I'd be thrilled to play what I've been practicing for you when I get back."

"Isn't that a lie?" Heather asked as she bundled up. "You told me you're not excited, you're scared."

Olivia's face grew red, but she held her head high. "Call it an exaggeration."

"Can't wait," Emma said, twiddling her fingers as Olivia and Heather disappeared out the back. The second the door slammed shut, she turned to Ethan and raised an eyebrow. "She's nice."

Ethan got up from the table, knowing he was incriminating himself by not answering. "What are you doing here, Emma? Really? Because a phone call would have sufficed if you wanted to check up on me."

Emma draped her arm over the back of the chair. "You hide too much over the phone. This way, I can look you in the eye and gauge your reactions for myself."

"Like I told you, I'm doing fine. Great, actually."

"Tell me, Ethan," Emma said, leaning across the table with her eyes trained on him and her lips curling into a smile. "How much of that has to do with Olivia?"

CHAPTER 8

"You'll do great," Ethan said, standing at the bottom of the steps for the temporary stage that'd been set up next to Holly Wreath's official Christmas tree. "If you do half as well as you played for Emma and me this morning, you'll blow this crowd away."

"I don't know," Olivia said as she surveyed the mass of people mingling around the tree, waiting for the ceremony to start. Fear was brewing in her gut, and she felt like she might lose the meager dinner she'd managed to eat. "I'm more nervous than a long tailed cat in a room full of rocking chairs."

"The worst part is over. You got through performing for the small group, which, in your own words, is harder than playing for the masses. Performing for the entire town of Holly Wreath should be a piece of cake, right?"

"Don't forget all the tourists who've come, too."

"Right. Them, too," Ethan said, standing on his tiptoes to try and get an estimate of how big the audience had gotten since they'd arrived. "There are probably fifteen hundred people here if I had to guess."

"You're really not helping," Olivia said in a clipped tone when her stomach flopped sickeningly.

Ethan's boyish smile distracted her from what was coming, and he put his hand on her shoulder, giving her a gentle shake to break her out of her spiraling nervousness. "Think of it as your chance to play at Carnegie Hall."

"And how is that supposed to help my stage fright?"

"Of all the people in the world, you have the opportunity to touch people's hearts this Christmas with your music. Doesn't that make you excited to share your gift with them?"

Olivia couldn't help but stare. It wasn't the first time she'd noticed his handsome features, from his straight nose to his defined jawline, but the hint of attraction she spied in his gaze caught her off guard. Her stomach jumped again, but instead of sick, it was a flurry of excitement as she dared to imagine the possibilities.

Olivia shifted on her feet and held her violin close to her chest, like the small amount of contact could give her a measure of warmth. Blowing out a lungful of air, her breath curled and dissipated into the cold night. "Sorry for snapping at you. You're right. I should think of this as an opportunity to bring others some Christmas cheer."

"I know it almost cracked my resolve to swear off Christmas forever listening to you play all week." Ethan winked, and Olivia had to look away to the Christmas tree to tame the ridiculous smile that was making her cheeks ache.

A gust of wind made Olivia retreat into her coat, though it did little to keep her from trembling. Putting her violin and bow under one arm, she reached for the hand warmers she had in her pockets to keep her fingers warm enough that she could play. If they turned into icicles, there was no way she'd be able to maneuver them over the strings. Glancing over at Ethan, her mind indulged her in a little reverie of

Ethan letting her put her arms around him for warmth, and him holding her in his strong arms in return.

Shaking herself out of her daydream, she looked at the microphone situated in the center of the stage, and an overwhelming shudder rattled down her spine. Ethan's eyebrows bunched together, and he dipped his head down to meet her gaze at her eye-level. "You're shivering."

"It's kind of hard not to. It is December in Wyoming."

"I'll give you that," Ethan agreed. "It might be nonstop rainy in Washington, but the temperatures are much more tepid."

"Always a tradeoff, huh?" Olivia bounced on her toes to try and produce some internal heat. "I can't totally blame the cold though. I shiver when I'm nervous too, so it'd pretty much be impossible for me to stand still right now, even if it was in the middle of summer and scorching hot."

"Let's see what we can at least do about the cold," Ethan said.

He'd borrowed a blanket off the back of Olivia's couch and had been using it to keep himself warm. Undoing his cocoon of blanket, he held open his arms and invited Olivia to step closer and do just what she'd been fantasizing. He vigorously rubbed his hands up and down her back while a nervous laughter bubbled out of Olivia. A previously untapped heat seeped through her veins, moving from her core all the way to the tips of her appendages.

"Does that help?" Ethan asked.

Olivia swallowed and squeaked, "Seems to be."

"Good," Ethan said. "If you need the blanket all to yourself, don't hesitate to tell me. I'm fine without it."

"This is perfect," Olivia said. Realizing the implication, she backpedaled. "I mean, it is nice. To be warm. It's nice to be warm with you." Olivia chewed on the inside of her cheek to try and get herself to stop. "I appreciate it."

The corners of Ethan's eyes began to crinkle as Olivia stumbled over her words. "Happy to help."

Her pulse was pounding so hard in her ears she almost didn't hear the mayor tap the microphone and welcome everyone to the tree lighting. He thanked the Holly Wreath Christmas Festival Committee who'd made the evening possible, then thanked Olivia for volunteering to accompany the singalong.

"Guilted into it is more like it," Olivia said, noticing she wasn't trembling anymore while she was pressed against Ethan's warmth and held by his steady hands.

Looking down at her, Ethan joked, "Volunteered. Guilted. It's all sort of the same thing, right?"

Olivia laughed. She wanted to lay her head on his chest, curious if his heart was hammering as hard as hers, but when the audience started clapping at the conclusion of the mayor's remarks, she knew her time had come.

Tightening his arms when she moved to step away, Ethan encouraged, "Just pretend you're playing in your living room just for me if that helps. This is your moment to shine."

Another shiver tickled her spine, but when Ethan pulled the flannel blanket off of her, she could hardly feel the biting cold of the nighttime air. Having been so close and feeling the draw to Ethan was enough to sustain her. With grace and poise, she took the stage, confidently waving once to the applauding crowd. Taking her position behind the microphone, she knew she was ready.

Putting her violin under her chin, she slowly raised her bow, inhaling and prepared to do her best. Closing her eyes, she played the opening strains of *Silent Night*, while a woman she'd seen on occasion in the diner stood nearby on the stage, conducting the audience as one enormous choir so they'd start singing on time.

After a brief introduction, the crowd was signaled to join

in. Tears filled Olivia's eyes as their words added beauty to the accompanying melody she provided with her violin. When she was younger, she had dreamed of having moments like these. Music had been a source of solace when she was worried or scared, but when Jeff had left, she'd lost a piece of her faith that life could ever hold happiness again. Because of that, she'd laid her music aside, overworked and overburdened by the worries of being a young single mother.

Opening her eyes, her gaze immediately found its way to where Ethan had joined Heather, Emma, and Twila. Heather was singing with abandon, while Twila and Emma watched with great amusement. Even though Ethan wasn't singing loudly, Olivia could see his lips moving along with the words. A feeling of love swelled within her, and the thought surprised her. She barely knew Ethan, but she knew she was falling for him.

At the end of the song, the lights of the tree flashed on, and the horde of people surrounding the tree collectively gasped before roaring with applause.

Olivia held the final note, and when she finished, the applause and whistles filled the whole of town square. Bowing with an enormous smile on her face, Olivia felt like she was on top of the world. She couldn't remember the last time Christmas wasn't full of pain over Jeff's betrayal or worry about how she was going to make ends meet while providing even a few meager gifts for Heather. As she stood on the stage, doing what fulfilled her, surrounded by the people and in the place she loved, she knew she was incredibly blessed.

With the tree lit, she accompanied the audience to two more upbeat Christmas carols before she gave one final bow. Skipping down the steps, she saw that Ethan was leading Heather, Emma, and Twila to reunite with her. In a moment of boldness, Olivia hurried to Ethan, pulling him into an embrace.

"Thank you," she said. "You don't know how much that means to me."

Quivering with adrenaline that moved through her, she felt emboldened by her accomplishment, so she kissed him on the cheek. He hesitated, shock written all over his face as he touched the place on his cheek where her lips had brushed his skin. When he regained his wits, he looped his arms around her, pulling her in close with a dopey grin that made his sister and Twila exchange a glance.

He cleared his throat and complimented, "You did fantastic."

Heather wriggled between Ethan and Olivia. "I didn't know you could play like that, Mom. It was really good."

Olivia kissed the top of her head. "Thanks, honey. I used to play for you all the time, but it's been a long time since I've performed for anybody. I'm sorry. I've been so busy, I sort of forgot how happy it makes me."

"No more excuses then," Heather said as she teasingly shook her pointer finger at her mother as she lectured. "You'll have to play every day so you don't forget."

Olivia giggled but agreed to her daughter's terms. When Heather ducked out from under Ethan and Olivia's arms, Olivia noticed he didn't let go completely, instead resting his hand on the small of her back. She didn't mind one bit.

"Congratulations," Emma said with a smirk that hid little of what she was thinking. "You did a wonderful job. It made fueling up the jet for an impromptu weekend here worth it."

Her mouth agape, Olivia asked, "You have a jet?"

Emma answered, "Don't you know—"

"It's a company plane," Ethan cut in. "It's not like it's parked in Emma's backyard or something."

"Right. Yeah. It's a company plane," Emma agreed, flapping her hand.

Twila squinted at them. "Where do you two work that you have a plane at your disposal?"

"You know," he said, stuffing his hands into his pockets and shrugging. "Just your regular corporate job. In the tech field."

"The tech field?" Twila parroted.

"Yeah. We're both in managerial positions, so that helps. Long hours, more perks," Ethan said.

"You can't be a day over thirty," Twila said as she appraised them.

Ethan shrugged. "We're good at what we do. Really good."

Twila huffed out a laugh. "I'd be willing to come out of retirement if those are the kinds of perks working folks are getting nowadays."

Emma blew warm air onto her fingers and stomped her feet. "I don't know about the rest of you, but I think my core temperature has dropped about five degrees since the sun went down. I need to warm up. You don't happen to have a hot tub, do you Olivia?"

"Sorry," Olivia said as she packed her violin back into its case, "that's an amenity that's still on the list for the inn. There is a nice big soaker tub in Ethan's bathroom if he'll let you borrow it."

Emma clasped her hands and looked pleadingly at her brother. He answered, "I don't know…"

Heather laughed at their sibling rivalry, clutching her sides as Emma screwed up her face with disgust. Swinging a fist at her brother, Emma said, "I can't believe you."

Ethan laughed and dodged her punch. "What are you going to give me?"

Emma wrapped her arms around herself and kept dancing from one foot to the other. "Nothing. I'm going to blackmail you with your deep, dark secrets until you give in. For example, do you know Ethan's middle name is—"

"Alright, alright," Ethan said, cupping his hand over Emma's mouth. "You win. Soak in my bathtub until your fingers are pruney."

Heather jumped up and down on her tiptoes and clapped. "What's his middle name? I wanna know."

"You'll have to guess," Ethan said. "I'd never willingly tell anyone."

"Um, Neville? George? Sheldon?" Heather said.

"Worse," Emma said, encouraging Heather's imagination.

Heather's lips twisted together while she thought. "Galileo?"

"Galileo?" Ethan laughed. "That would be a sweet middle name."

"Well, what is it then?" Heather asked with pleading puppy dog eyes.

Olivia straightened Heather's knit hat, and tugged on the strings. "It's probably something really awful, like, I don't know…Barnabas."

Ethan's eyes widened, and Emma tried to hide her laughter behind her hand until she looked like she'd burst at the seams. Tears ran down her cheeks, and she asked, "How'd you guess?"

"I'm right?" Olivia asked, doing a double take. "Your middle name is Barnabas?"

Sheepishly, Ethan nodded. "It's one of those distinguished family names. I guess I should be glad that I'm not Barnabas the fourth, like my grandfather wanted me to be."

"I suppose you could have gone by Barnie," Twila said, sticking her tongue out as she giggled.

Covering his eyes with his hand, Ethan groaned, "Somehow that doesn't sound any better."

"As much as I'd love to stay here and razz Ethan, I'm with

Emma. It's getting downright chilly out here. Why don't we go back to the inn and warm up with some hot chocolate?" Olivia offered. "The wood burning stove is probably still warm."

"We can keep teasing Ethan there," Heather said as she sniggered. "Barnabas…"

Clapping his hands together, Ethan said, "I've been wanting another cup of your hot chocolate. Doesn't tonight seem like a good night to celebrate?"

"I've heard of your legendary hot chocolate," Emma said. "Do you put whipped cream on top?"

"Full fat cream all the way," Olivia said.

Emma closed her eyes and moaned. "Don't tell me what's in it or I might talk myself out of it."

"You're not a health nut like Ethan, are you?" Olivia asked. "I'll be the first to admit I'm not great at cooking without calories."

"Not a health nut but let's just say I don't metabolize nearly as effortlessly as you seem to," Emma said.

"You can drink your hot chocolate in ignorant bliss," Ethan said. "Olivia's going to go to the grave with her hot chocolate recipe."

"Nah, I'll pass it onto Heather when she's ready," Olivia said, making her daughter beam with pride. "I will tell you I don't hold back on the fat though. It'd be wrong."

"I'll have to take your word for it," Emma said, putting her hand on her stomach. "At least I already fit into my wedding dress."

Heather lost her patience and grabbed Ethan and Olivia's hands. "Come on, then!"

They wormed their way through the crowd in a single-file line, Olivia accepting accolades as people she knew congratulated her on her violin performance, and every one of them mentioned they never suspected she played.

"See?" Ethan said when they made it out of the fray of people.

"See what?" Olivia asked, bumping shoulders with him as they walked.

"I told you people were going to love you," Ethan said.

He opened the passenger door for her, and she slid in, feeling her cheeks burning at the way he looked at her. Olivia was sure Twila and Emma noticed, but Olivia herself was surprised it didn't bother her. She was a grown woman and deserved her shot at love as much as the next girl.

Everyone got into Ethan's rental car, and they drove slowly through Holly Wreath, weaving their way through the heavy foot traffic and admiring the lights on the houses, making the dark winter night feel more cheerful and bright.

Ethan parked in the driveway, and everyone rushed inside, dropping their coats and scarves on chairs and congregating around the wood burning stove. Emma skipped up the stairs two at a time to start filling the tub in Ethan's room, while Ethan volunteered to bring in an armful of logs to revive the coals of the wood burning stove.

Making sure the fire was going on its own, Olivia shut the door and stood up, dusting off her hands.

Emma floated down the stairs in a silk robe and leaned on the banister. "Do you happen to have any candles? I like my bubble baths in lowlight."

Heather turned around on the couch, and her mouth fell open. "What's your robe made of? It looks so soft and shiny."

"You like it?" Emma said, striking a pose. "It's silk."

"Silk? Isn't silk expensive?" Heather asked.

Emma tightened the belt of her robe. "It's worth it."

"Ethan already told me you guys are really rich," Heather said. She pulled a flannel blanket off the back of the couch and snuggled up in the corner. "How much money do you have?"

"Heather," Olivia chided, looking at Ethan to gauge whether or not he was offended. "That's rude."

"What?" Heather said, genuinely confused.

"It's alright. Being accused of having money isn't the worst thing in the world," Emma said as she descended the rest of the stairs and leaned against the ornate newel post at the bottom of the steps.

"As long as it doesn't turn into your obsession," Olivia interjected.

Emma put her hand on her waist and countered, "Money isn't bad, Olivia."

"Money isn't bad. *Obsessing* over money has ruined plenty of families, and broken a lot of homes," Olivia said. She knew she was being a terrible hostess, but the topic was one she was hopelessly passionate about.

Instead of being offended, Emma laughed with great humor, letting Olivia breathe easier. "I'll give you that."

"Let me get you those candles," Olivia said.

Olivia rummaged through the linen closet for spare candles and sent Emma off to take a bath. Then Olivia excused herself to unwind in the kitchen. It'd been a long day, but making hot chocolate for everyone under her roof was the only way she could adequately thank them for their support.

"It'll take me a while to get everything ready for the hot chocolate," Olivia announced. "Twenty minutes or so. Make yourselves at home."

In the kitchen, she tied on her apron and started getting pots out to simmer the hot chocolate to perfection. She worked in a flurry, measuring milk and cream, stirring it together in a large stockpot with sugar, and a dash of cinnamon.

"Anything I can help with?"

Olivia squeaked and jumped at the intrusion. "Ethan!

You've got to quit doing that, or I'm going to die of a heart attack right here in my own kitchen."

"That'd be too bad. I was really hoping for another cup of your hot chocolate before you go."

Olivia swatted at him with her wooden spoon. "I kind of get lost in my thoughts in here when I'm fixin' to make something."

"Fixin'? Your southern roots are beginning to show again."

Olivia clicked her tongue and turned her attention back to the stove to make sure the milk and cream didn't scorch. "No, I don't need help with anything. You go sit down and relax. You're a guest in this house, which I suppose you've forgotten since I ran you ragged this week."

When the milk and cream began to steam, Olivia poured in a tablespoon of vanilla and stirred, then made sure the whipped chocolate was ready to be added. Glancing over her shoulder, she saw that Ethan hadn't budged from his spot.

Pretending to block the stove, she teasingly warned, "I'm going to have to wrestle you out of the kitchen myself if you don't leave. I'm not kidding. I've never shared this hot chocolate recipe with anyone."

Ethan smiled but still didn't move. His throat bobbed up and down as he swallowed, and the way he looked at Olivia made her own mouth go dry.

"What?" she asked, feeling around with her fingertips. "Do I have chocolate on my face?"

"No."

Smoothing her hand over her hair, she said, "Please don't tell me now that my hair has been messed up since the tree lighting."

"Your hair looks beautiful."

"Then what is it? Because I wasn't kidding when I said I'd chase out anyone who came nosing around the kitchen."

Olivia swung her wooden spoon back and forth a couple of times for good measure.

Running a hand across the scruff on his cheeks, the way he looked at her with his gorgeous hazel eyes was hypnotizing. "I really hope I'm not totally out of line, but I was wondering if maybe you'd consider going out with me."

Olivia almost dropped her spoon but fumbled to catch it. "You? And me? As in, a date?"

Ethan grinned, and it was so charming it made Olivia's heart ache. "That's kind of the idea, yeah. A date."

"When?"

"How about tomorrow night. I'd love to give you a night off. We could go to dinner."

A girlish giggle escaped Olivia, and the flurry of butterflies she'd felt earlier in the night was nothing compared to the stampede of flutters rippling through her insides.

Trying to keep her cool to avoid looking desperate, Olivia beamed. "A date with you would be the best Christmas present I could ask for."

CHAPTER 9

"How does this look?"

Ethan came out of the large walk-in closet where he'd put on the suit he'd worn on his way into Holly Wreath, when he couldn't take the pressure of his life in Seattle and had had to escape. Paired with a pale blue shirt and a silk tie, he was ready to spend a very different evening with Olivia than he had before.

Emma stood up from the armchair where she had been filing her nails while she waited. Brushing off his lapels, she straightened his tie without answering.

"Too much?" Ethan asked.

Emma chuckled. "You're taking her to a nice restaurant, aren't you?"

"The only five-star in all of Holly Wreath," Ethan said as he sat down on the bench at the end of his bed to put on his shoes.

"I think you'll be fine. You should see the dress Olivia picked out," Emma said. "She's just as anxious about this date as you are."

Ethan clenched his jaw, ruminating over the complicated

bundle of emotions that were coming at him like a tidal wave. "Where'd you take her shopping?"

"I asked her where the nicest stores in Holly Wreath were, and she drove me to this cute little collection of boutique shops. Why?"

Ethan scrubbed a hand down his face. "Emma. You can't keep doing that."

Emma pointed a finger to her chest. "Me? What?"

"Rubbing it in her face that we have money, because if it isn't obvious to you, Olivia doesn't."

"I bought her a nice dress. So what?"

"And came home with ten bags of things for yourself. Don't think I didn't see you hiding them in your room."

"I was Christmas shopping. It was nice to have different shops to choose from. Then it was easier to convince Olivia it was no big deal to get her a new dress since I was buying stuff for myself anyway. Besides, Heather was on my side."

"That may be, and your heart might be in the right place, but I think you're forgetting who we are. We're two of the wealthiest people in the entire country."

"Are you afraid Olivia's going to be interested in your money the way Mallory was?"

"No. Yes. I don't know. I do know that she already has her own issues with it. That's one of the reasons her husband left her and Heather. Money's sort of a sore subject."

"Oh. I didn't know." Emma looked queasy. "I hate it when people get lucky and strike it rich, then think they're better than the people who helped get them there."

"It was worse, Emma. They were so poor that they used her college fund to try and start this bed and breakfast, and when the money didn't roll in like he thought it should, he split."

Emma put her hand over her forehead. "I'm such an idiot. I get why you kept giving me all those nasty looks now."

"I'm not blaming you. Just don't rub in that we have a private business jet and that your wedding ring is the size of a small glacier."

"And you're sure she doesn't know already? That you're *the* Ethan Wilder? You were just on the cover of *Forbes.*"

"I don't think she has time to read *Forbes,*" Ethan said with a teasing smirk.

"I've occasionally seen you on less reputable magazines, too."

Ethan looked at himself in the full length mirror hanging on the closet door. "I don't take her for the type who reads the grocery aisle trashy magazines, either. Besides, if she does suspect me, she hasn't said anything. You have to give her credit for that."

"Oh, definitely. From what I can tell, she's a great lady, and Heather is a doll." Emma hesitated, and Ethan knew she was holding back what was really on her mind.

"Go ahead. Spit it out."

Emma sat down next to him. "I just don't want to see you get hurt again. And so soon after what Mallory did."

"I'm fine."

Emma studied his face, then satisfied he was telling the truth, she stood and walked to the door. "Good. Because I actually *really* like Olivia. I don't want to see you screw it up."

Ethan laughed at his sister. "Thanks for the vote of confidence."

"Hey," she said, grabbing the door knob, "you of all people have to know how grumpy you can be."

"I'm also a lot of fun."

Emma rolled her eyes. "If you say so. You're going to come clean though, right?"

Scoffing, Ethan answered, "My financial status isn't something I'm ashamed of."

"Then why are you trying to hide it?" Ethan hated it when Emma raised her eyebrows like she did.

"I'm not. It's something I think should be mentioned at the right time," Ethan said. "If anything, I'm concerned the celebrity part of my life will be off-putting. There's a certain level of attention I get, and Olivia's a pretty private person."

Emma nodded. "Alright. I trust you not to mess it up."

"I'm holding you to that."

"I'm going to go see if Olivia needs any help getting ready." Emma opened the door and stepped out.

"Be down in a minute."

After she shut the door, he could hear Emma's footsteps trotting down the steps and muted voices coming from the living room. Grabbing his wallet, he tucked it in his pocket and made sure he had his keys and phone when he felt his phone buzz.

Taking it out, he checked to make sure it wasn't something from his secretary. Peg was great about filtering the things for him, so only the most urgent reached him when he needed some time away, but even she couldn't do some things. Turning on the screen his blood felt like an icy river in the depths of winter.

It was a text from Mallory.

Ethan, baby. I've missed you.

Ethan had to sit down when his legs threatened to give way. He'd suspected Mallory would eventually come slinking back to him, though he thought she might have had the decency to be apologetic when she did. At one time, he'd even considered giving her a second chance. Their match made sense on paper. It would've been good for both their families, and she was the kind of woman that would've looked good hanging onto his arm at charity dinners and new product announcement galas.

That was before he met Olivia.

Another text came in, and Ethan couldn't help himself from looking.

C'mon, Ethan. I know you're there.

Ethan's heart about beat out of his chest as he typed and erased, then typed and erased again. Another text came from Mallory.

We need to talk. Answer me.

Her boldness irritated Ethan, and his fingers flew as he typed:

I'm busy right now.

It took barely any time for Mallory to answer.

Sure you are. At work?

Her unremorseful approach to striking up a text conversation with him rubbed him the wrong way. He answered:

I'm not in Seattle right now.

From the bottom of the steps, Emma shouted up to him. "Are you ready, Ethan? Your reservation is in twenty minutes!"

"Just a sec," he called down through the door.

His phone vibrated again with Mallory's answer:

Where are you?

Ethan felt a bit devious as he typed out his reply:

On a date.

He smiled to himself and tossed his phone back onto his bed. It was a bit cruel of him to leave Mallory wondering what exactly he'd meant, but he wasn't in the mood for her dramatics. She deserved to feel some of the pain she'd caused him. He'd answer her when he got back from his date with Olivia.

Maybe.

Ethan felt like a feather, drifting down the stairs without a care in the world. He was finally free of Mallory's controlling influence, and he wanted nothing more than to take Olivia out on a date, show her a good time, and get to know her. He had no idea if she kissed on first dates or not, but he wouldn't complain one bit if the chance arose.

"Took you long enough," Emma said, reaching up to fix his hair.

He swatted her away. "I had some…business come up."

Emma's eyebrows shot up. "Business or business *with* someone in particular…?"

Before Ethan could answer, Olivia caught his attention over Emma's shoulder. She was a vision in a red dress that hit right above her knees and black booties and tights to keep her warm. Shyly, she peeked at him as she pushed her hair behind her ear.

Heather came skipping out behind her and stopped right by Ethan. "Doesn't she look pretty?"

Ethan nodded. "I was actually thinking the word was stunning."

"That works, too," Heather said.

Olivia rubbed her red-tinted lips together and touched the small pearl-drop earring dangling from her earlobe. "It's not too much?"

"No," Ethan reassured her. "You look amazing."

Emma raised her hand. "Heather and I have to take some credit for Olivia's apparel. If it were up to her, she would've worn a pair of overalls and a flannel shirt."

Olivia shrugged. "What's wrong with being practical?"

"Because, Mom," Heather said matter-of-factly. "This is a special occasion. It calls for a special outfit."

Emma got their coats out of the closet and handed them both to Ethan. He helped Olivia slip hers on, while asking Heather, "You're sure you don't want to go with us? I wouldn't mind one bit if you came, too."

Heather scrunched up her nose. "I've heard of the place you're eating. Someone at my school went there with her parents, and she said it was all slimy clams and stinky cheeses. No, thank you."

"Besides," Emma said, wrapping her arm around Heather's neck and pulling her over, "it's girl's night in for us. We're going to do nails and watch a cheesy chick flick and eat way too much ice cream."

"You don't mind staying with Heather?" Olivia said.

"On the contrary," Emma said. "I'm really looking forward to it."

Heather leaned into Emma. "We're besties. Now go! I'm ready to eat ice cream until I'm sick since you won't be here to stop me."

Heather and Emma shooed them out the door. Ethan kept his hand on the small of her back, guiding her to the passenger side of his rental. He had the car unlocked and running, and she slid into the seat, thanking him for getting the door.

The drive to Maison de Fleur was quiet and slow and

Ethan didn't mind the lack of conversation. There was comfort in existing with each other without the need to fill it with words, even though he could tell Olivia was nervous. She looked out the window at the passing Christmas lights and displays on the houses while her hands had a mind of their own, fidgeting in her lap. Ethan turned on the radio to find some Christmas music, hoping it would help her relax.

Olivia looked to him and smiled. "You're starting to make me think you're not as much of a Scrooge as you profess you are."

"Says the lady who serenaded the entire town to the most beautiful rendition of *Silent Night* that anyone's ever heard."

Olivia tucked her hands under her legs. "I don't blame Christmas for anything, remember? It's just usually this time of year—the cold, the smells…it has the tendency to bring up memories I'd rather forget. Besides, you said this season has been particularly unhappy for you, which is why you were a grump when I met you. Is that still true?"

Ethan slowed the car to a stop at a red light and stared at Olivia. Her blue eyes were expectant, and her mouth looked especially kissable as she caught her lower lip between her teeth.

"I can honestly say this has been the happiest Christmas season I've ever had," Ethan said in a low voice.

"Good." Olivia gave him a faint smile but her gaze had dropped down to his lips, too.

It might have been a while since he kissed anyone other than Mallory—and even they had hardly so much as given each other a peck on the cheek the last year, unless they were in public and people expected something more—but the thought of kissing Olivia seemed so right.

He slowly leaned over, and she closed her eyes, her breathing becoming shallow and rapid. When he was so close that he could feel the electricity between them, the car behind them honked and flashed their brights.

The two of them snapped apart, red in the face and flustered at their almost-kiss, and Ethan drove through the intersection as the light turned yellow.

"Sorry," Olivia muttered, staring out the window again and playing with a strand of hair that was curled in front of her ear. "I'm rushing things."

Ethan laughed and reached over to pick up her hand. "I'm the one who did the leaning in."

Olivia laced her fingers through his, and he squeezed her hand, which fit so well in his. Her hand was calloused and strong and told the story of how hard she worked. It was a small detail most people would miss about Olivia unless they paid very close attention to her. He considered himself grateful he had the time to notice.

She looked back over to him, and there was a mischievous sparkle in her eye. "Then we'll have to assume it wasn't meant to be. Yet."

Ethan's insides lurched, feeling like the thrilling drop of a roller coaster, and he determined he was going to kiss Olivia Campbell before the night was over. He put little stock in luck, and instead would make sure the timing was impeccable.

Pulling over to the valet, Ethan got out and handed the keys along with a generous tip, folded into his hand as he shook the valet's so Olivia wouldn't notice. He may have had money, but he didn't want to give the impression he was showing off.

"I've lived here for almost ten years, and I've never eaten here," Olivia said as they walked into the restaurant.

"That's too bad," Ethan said, looking around to soak it all in. "It seems like a nice place."

The lights were dim, and there was quiet piano music

seasoning the atmosphere between the hushed conversation. As many tables as were situated in the open space, they were almost all full, mostly with couples who leaned in toward each other, talking and sharing bites of food. It was exactly the kind of place Ethan had hoped it'd be for their first date.

Sitting down and accepting their menus from the hostess, Ethan unfolded his napkin and set it across his lap.

Olivia opened her menu and her eyes widened slightly. "Nice usually has a price tag."

Ethan reached over and pulled down the top of her menu so he could see her. "Don't worry about the cost. It's irrelevant tonight. In fact, let's play a game."

"A game?" Olivia said, quirking her head to the side. "What kind of game?"

Ethan tugged the menu from her hands and set it next to him. "You tell me what you're in the mood for, and I'll order for the both of us. Then you won't have to worry about anything except whether or not I have good taste in food."

Olivia raised an eyebrow. "Am I going to end up eating slimy clams and stinky cheeses like Heather's friend said?"

Ethan shrugged and tightened his lips. "That all depends on if you trust me or not."

"Alright." Olivia sat back against the booth. "I'll play your game."

"So," Ethan said, opening up the menu and doing a quick scan. "What'll it be?"

Tapping her chin, Olivia said, "I guess I'd like something that's hearty but not too heavy. I like a touch of spice but nothing that'll burn off my taste buds. Bonus points if it's sweet and savory."

Ethan nodded as he skimmed the menu, deciding on what to get her. The waiter took their drink orders, and when he came back with ice waters and a sparkling cranberry Christmas drink along with a basket of assorted breads,

Ethan put in an order by pointing to the menu while the waiter scribbled it down.

"Very good, sir," the waiter said, taking the menus from Ethan. "Your food will be out shortly."

"That was secretive," Olivia said, selecting a honey wheat roll and tearing off a piece. "Is covert your normal mode of operation?"

Ethan took a sip of his water and shrugged. "I've got lots of secrets. But that's kind of the adventure of a relationship, isn't it? Finding out all about each other?"

"I suppose," Olivia agreed. "I feel like we've spent a lot of time together, with you helping me get a good start on the final guest bedroom and having your sister visit—"

"In my defense, you can't really take anything my sister says as gospel truth. She embellishes and exaggerates more than she thinks she does."

"I'll remember that. Still, all that time together this week and I don't even think I've scratched the surface of who you really are."

"Then go ahead," Ethan leaned back, stretching his arms across the back of the booth. "Shoot."

"Alright," Olivia said, her playful eyes catching the light of the candle flickering between them, "If you could be an animal, what would you be and why?"

Ethan shook his head while he chuckled. "Going right for the big questions, aren't you?"

"I already know your middle name, and I figure this is a way of psychoanalyzing you, the way you did in ordering food for me."

Ethan laughed again as the waiter came over with their meals. Setting down their plates, Olivia's eyes danced with delight as she was given a braised pork chop with cranberry sauce, roasted red fingerling potatoes, and a berry and pine nut salad.

Slicing off a piece of her pork, her eyes rolled back in her head and she moaned with satisfaction. "This is so good. You hit the nail on the head, Ethan. Well done."

"I did alright then?"

She took another bite and nodded. "It's like heaven on a plate."

"Good," Ethan said, spearing a bite of his lobster. "I passed the test."

Wiping her mouth with her napkin, she said, "You did. Heather's going to be disappointed she missed this."

"I think she'll be alright. Emma has a sweet tooth that can't be rivaled, and she'll probably let Heather eat her weight in junk food."

"True," Olivia said, matching Ethan's smile. It warmed his heart to see Olivia so carefree and content, and in that moment, he realized that all he wanted was to make Olivia happy. "So? What kind of animal?"

Ethan had to think for a moment. "I guess I'd like to be a bird. I imagine it's incredible to fly. You?"

Narrowing her eyes while she thought, she poked her fork in his direction. "I'd want to be a dolphin. They always look like they're having so much fun."

While they ate, they came up with increasingly difficult questions for each other, and together, they laughed. It was definitely the most entertaining evening he'd had in a long time.

"Alright, my turn," Olivia said, finishing off the last of her food. "What's your favorite Christmas memory?"

The question caught him off guard, and he sat back in his seat, combing through his memories to see if he even had any good feelings about the season. He'd spent so long trying to ignore it as much as he could that he wasn't sure he'd ever really let himself enjoy it.

"I guess, it would have been when I was in school. There was this girl I liked, and she kissed me under the mistletoe."

"Oh," Olivia said. Her countenance sank. "I guess that's memorable."

Ethan couldn't contain his laughter, and it came sputtering out. "If it makes you feel better, it was when I was in first grade, and the girl carried around a sprig of mistletoe in her pocket so she could kiss whatever boy she felt like that day."

Olivia's shock gave way to laughter, and the two of them clutched their sides as tears rolled down their cheeks while other patrons gave them funny looks.

"Okay," Olivia said, dabbing her napkin at the tears on her cheeks, "you got me. I was worried that I was out on a date with a player."

"I felt a bit betrayed by her methods when I found out, too. I've tried to be much more careful in love since then."

Olivia gazed at him, and his heart did a flip in his chest. He couldn't get over how beautiful she looked with her hair down, dressed up, and without the stress and strain of worry on her face that she'd had when he'd first met her. Reaching across the table, he took her hand.

"What's your favorite Christmas memory?" Ethan asked.

"That's easy," she said, sitting up straighter in her seat. "Every year, I've loved having Heather knock on my door so early on Christmas morning that the stars are still out. She does it so we can go into the living room together. The expression on her face when she realizes Santa hasn't forgotten her makes my heart happy. She never complains when our pile of presents is small, and that innocence, joy and wonder that only a child can have at Christmastime helps me forget that there ever was anything sad in the world, at least for the day."

Olivia's gaze dropped down to her empty plate, and Ethan was sure she was trying to blink back tears.

"Hey, what's the matter? That sounds like a wonderful Christmas memory," he said.

Olivia sniffled and half-laughed while tears began trickling down her face. "It is. It's just…oh, I'm so silly. Remember how I told you not to say anything to Heather about Santa? I think she's getting too old for it. She's been asking questions, and I don't want to outright lie…"

Ethan finished for her. "You're worried that happy part of Christmas might be ending?"

Dabbing the tears off her face, she took in a deep breath and put a smile back on her face. "Exactly. I don't know what there will be left of Christmas if I don't have that one small joy watching Heather savor the holiday."

"It makes sense," Ethan said.

The waiter stopped by to fill up their waters and carry off their plates so he could set down a decadent slice of Black Forest gateau for them to share. Olivia took a bite, licking her lips at the richness of the cake. "I'm not sure I could take another bite. I'm stuffed."

"We'll take it home," Ethan said.

Home. He knew he was still paying to stay in Olivia's bed and breakfast, but as the days had passed, the quaint house he'd gotten to know so well as he worked side by side with Olivia, the place that was always full of good food, warmth, and companionship had begun to feel very much like the feeling of home he'd been missing for so long.

"I'd like that," Olivia said, sitting back and sighing.

Ethan's leg began to jiggle under the table as he pondered Olivia's worries, and the implications of Heather no longer believing in Santa.

"Olivia, I know you're worried that Christmas might not

be the same without Heather believing in Santa Claus, but I don't think it'll ruin it for her."

"Is that so?" Olivia said with a skeptical tilt of her head. "Do tell."

"Obviously, she's not going to stay naïve forever. The question is how she's going to find out."

"I know. I should probably tell her before some playground bully spoils it for her."

"Yes, but also, I think you can instill in her the ideals that make Santa so appealing."

Olivia crossed one leg over the other and rested her ankles next to his, making his skin tingle at the touch. "What do you mean?"

"Well, think about it. What is it that people like about Santa?"

"To a child? I suppose it's the gifts, the wonder of being surprised, the thought that they're special enough for someone else who everyone loves, loves them in return."

"Isn't that the same for everyone? It's kind of the essence of Christmas," Ethan said, giving Olivia's hand a squeeze.

"That and that we're celebrating the birth of the Savior," Olivia said. She winked teasingly at Ethan, and he couldn't help but laugh.

"That part definitely tops it, but I think giving gifts aligns with celebrating His birth, too. I'm not a father by any means, so correct me if you think I'm wrong, but I think if you explained it to Heather and told her that now she's old enough to be one of the people who carries on the spirit of Old Saint Nick, that maybe, you'll still get to see a lot of what makes Christmas special."

Olivia mulled over his words, and when she finally nodded, she looked like a weight had been lifted off her shoulders. "You're probably right. She's going to find out one way or another. At least this way I get to be the one controlling the circumstances, and hopefully it won't be too much of a blow to her. I just don't want it to be a letdown, you know?"

"Heather's a very resilient girl," Ethan said. "She's got a lot of her spunk from you."

"No argument there," Olivia said with a snort.

"If you'd like, I could be there when you break the news. Maybe tomorrow morning over a big breakfast?"

"I'd like that," Olivia said.

The way Olivia looked at him, with such relief and appreciation, Ethan could have lived in that moment forever. He'd all but forgotten about Mallory and how lukewarm their relationship had been, even at its best. Comparing it to the potential he could glimpse with Olivia, there was no question what path he should take.

The bill came, and the rest of their cake was packaged up to go home with them. Back out in the cold, Olivia stood close to him while they waited for the valet, dancing to keep herself warm. Wrapping his arm across her shoulders, he pulled her in close, breathing in her gentle scent.

Over Olivia's head, Ethan noticed a tall brunette with a leopard print coat looking at him, pointing him out to the group of women she was standing with. He didn't recognize her, but she was staring so intently that it made him wonder if he'd been found out, and his quiet, undisturbed time of inconspicuousness in Holly Wreath was coming to an end.

The valet brought the car around, and after he helped Olivia in, he saw the woman had her phone out and was snapping photos of him. Ducking into the car, his heart hammered against his ribs, and he pulled out onto the street faster than he needed to. He was no stranger to people ambushing him, taking photos when he least expected it so they could post them on social media, bragging about spotting him.

Pulling into the driveway, he put the BMW in park and

peered at the old Holly Wreath Inn. It was in need of a paint job, and the shingles on the roof were starting to curl, but the same feeling of safety, security, and love he'd had at the restaurant washed over him again. He had Olivia to thank for that.

"Thanks for the lovely evening," Olivia said, demurely meeting his eyes.

"I was going to say the same to you. I had a lot of fun getting to know you in a different way."

"If you don't mind, I think there's one thing we need to finish to make this evening absolutely perfect."

Ethan's heart rate revved as Olivia focused on him. "Yeah? What's that?"

A slow smile curled the edges of Olivia's mouth, and she leaned in closer, her nose almost touching his. "How about that kiss?"

CHAPTER 10

"Pass the raisins, please," Heather said, pointing to the small, paisley-painted ceramic bowl on Ethan's side of the table.

He picked it up and handed it over. "I've never heard of anyone putting raisins in their oatmeal before."

"Really?" Heather dumped half the bowl on top of her oatmeal, she picked out a few and tossed them into her mouth. "They're so good."

"Not a fan, I guess," Ethan said.

"You're missing out then," Olivia said. "My granny always used to put raisins in our porridge before she sprinkled it with brown sugar and cinnamon. Sometimes, she'd give us a scoop of ice cream to cool it down, too."

"At that point, you might as well have cake for breakfast," Ethan joked, taking a bite of his breakfast. He'd barely added a touch of honey to sweeten it and had asked if she had any frozen blueberries, otherwise eating it plain. Olivia had to hand it to him for enjoying his healthy breakfast without the embellishments she'd set out on the table. Her sweet tooth had been nagging her all morning, and she decided to indulge it.

Olivia licked her lips at the mention of cake and pretended to drool, making Heather giggle. "You wouldn't have to try and convince me to eat breakfast cake."

"Me, neither," Heather said. "So why don't we make some now?"

"Because," Olivia said, cupping Heather's cheeks in her hands, "if I let you have whatever you wanted, you'd regret it later, especially when all your teeth rot from all that sugar."

"Can I have cake for breakfast on my birthday?" Heather asked, batting her eyelashes.

Olivia and Ethan both laughed at Heather's theatrics, and Olivia answered, "You know I'll make an exception on your birthday. I always do."

"What the birthday girl wants, the birthday girl gets," Heather said as she scooped a too-large spoonful of oatmeal into her mouth.

"Right," Olivia agreed, "but since your birthday's not for five more months, there's no point in asking about it today. Now eat up. We're going to be late for church."

"Are you coming, Ethan?" Heather asked, washing down her oatmeal with a drink of milk.

"Sure," Ethan said with a one-shouldered shrug. "I'd love to."

Olivia smiled at Heather, grateful she'd asked the question Olivia had been trying to find the bravery to ask, not because she was embarrassed she was a church-goer, but because she didn't want Ethan to feel awkward or pressured. Heather's forwardness and unbeguiling nature bypassed all those concerns.

"Then you'd better eat up, too," Olivia said.

Heather looked over her shoulder, down the hallway to the stairs. "Where's your sister?"

Ethan followed her gaze. "I think you must've worn her out last night."

"Me? Hardly. She's the one who made me stay up late to watch another movie with her," Heather said. "I ended up falling asleep on the couch, and she had to poke me to wake me up when you guys got home."

"I'm just teasing you, Heather," Ethan said as his eyes glimmered happily. "Emma is a notorious late sleeper and will sleep till noon if she gets the chance."

"She's welcome to sleep in as late as she wants. That's part of the privilege of being a paying guest at the Holly Wreath Inn," Olivia said, bringing over a pitcher of orange juice.

She sat down next to Ethan, her heart melting like a popsicle on a hot summer day when he smiled at her and brushed his leg against hers under the table. The memory of the goodnight kiss they'd shared at the end of their date the night before popped into her head, and she could feel her cheeks flushing uncontrollably.

"Are you alright, Mom?" Heather asked, watching her over her breakfast. "You look...sweaty."

Olivia ignored the urge to fan herself and stood up to get the cinnamon sugar out of the spice drawer. "I was thinking about something. From last night."

She turned around, and judging by the grin on Ethan's face, their kiss was fresh in his mind, too.

Before Heather suspected anything, Ethan swooped in and mercifully changed the subject. "That reminds me, Olivia. Don't you have something you wanted to bring up this morning?"

Ethan winked conspicuously and nodded toward Heather. Scooping in another spoonful of oatmeal, Heather asked, "Is there something in your eye?"

"Heather," Olivia warned, pinching her own lips shut in demonstration. "Manners."

Heather swallowed and looked sheepishly at her mother. "Sorry."

Olivia slid into her chair and placed her hand over Heather's. Under the table, she felt Ethan's hand slide into hers in encouragement. Sandwiched between the two of them, Olivia felt complete and comfortable, something she hadn't experienced in a very long time.

Heather's brown eyes shifted between Olivia and Ethan. "What's going on? You're both acting weird."

Olivia's contentedness didn't last long. At Heather's question, it felt like someone had poured a pitcher of ice water over her head while she tried to figure out how to come clean about the legend of Santa Claus. The last thing Olivia wanted was to totally crush her daughter and ruin Christmas by going about revealing Santa's fictitious nature in the wrong way.

"Heather, I've been meaning to talk to you for a while…"

"About what?" Heather licked clean her spoon. "Wait. Are you two dating now?"

"What? No," Olivia said, her eyes darting over to Ethan and her stress levels rose through the roof. "We went on *a* date. That doesn't mean we're dating, sweetie."

Ethan spoke up. "I do think your mom is a fantastic woman, but that's not what she wanted to talk to you about, no."

Heather looked more confused by the minute. "Then what is it?"

"Honey," Olivia said, tracing the flower pattern on the tablecloth with her finger, "I wanted to talk to you about Christmas."

"Christmas?" Heather parroted. "What about it?"

"Not so much Christmas, but Santa Claus."

Olivia watched her daughter, trying to gauge what she was thinking. At the slightest hint of distress, she was going to abandon the conversation and let her believe in Santa as long as she wanted.

"What about him?" Heather asked.

"Well," Olivia said, "you know how we've talked about how sometimes history starts with a believable event, but as time has passed, the story becomes more embellished?"

"Yeah," Heather said. "And?"

Olivia couldn't seem to sit still as she searched for the words. Her eyes stung with surprise tears, and she wasn't sure she wanted to go through with her confession. She wanted Heather to enjoy one more year of blissful ignorance and innocence. Her life had been hard enough as the daughter of a single mother, and in some ways, Heather had already had to grow up faster than she should've had to.

"Mom," Heather asked, "are you trying to break it to me that Santa's not real?"

Olivia blinked, and her mouth opened. She looked to Ethan, wondering if he'd secretly told her so Olivia wouldn't have to be the one to break the news.

He held up his hands like Olivia was holding him at gunpoint. "Don't look at me."

Satisfied Ethan wasn't the culprit, Olivia said, "Yeah, actually. How'd you know that he's not real?"

Heather dropped her spoon into her bowl and laced her fingers together, leaning her elbows on the top of the table. "I figured it out last year when I saw that puppy dog toy in the store and told you I wanted it for Christmas. You forgot to take off the price sticker, and I saw it when I unwrapped it."

Olivia put her hand over her eyes and massaged her temples. "I'm sorry. I ruined Santa Claus for you."

Feeling a hand on her back, Olivia peeked between her fingers to see Heather smiling at her. "It's alright, Mom. I would have figured it out sooner or later, especially since there's this boy in my class that keeps telling everyone Santa's not real."

Olivia sat up straighter. "Tell me who it is, and I'll talk to the principal."

"No, Mom. It's okay." Heather sat back down in her seat. "Nobody believes anything that kid says, anyway."

Olivia took in a breath that filled every inch of her lungs, then blew it out through her lips in a loud sigh. "So you're not upset?"

"Do I still get presents?" Heather asked.

Ethan chuckled while Olivia smiled at Heather's eagerness. "Yes. Of course. That part of Christmas doesn't change."

"Then yeah, I'm fine. It's still fun to pretend," Heather said as swung her legs under the table.

"It is," Olivia agreed. "In fact, that's what I like most about Christmas. I get to carry on the spirit of Santa by being the one who surprises you."

Ethan said, "That's what Emma and I get to do every Christmas, too. We have a charity and part of its purpose is we give gifts to underprivileged children during the holidays."

Olivia raised an eyebrow. "You have a charity?"

Taking a sip of his juice, Ethan shrugged and wiped his lips. "Through the company, technically."

"Ah," Olivia said with a nod, feeling a twinge of jealousy that he got to help people on that scale. Never admitting it to anyone, Olivia thought she'd make a fantastic philanthropist, having experienced poverty firsthand. "That must be very fulfilling."

"It is," Ethan agreed. "But it isn't any less special when one person does it for another. It's not the amount that's given, but the act of giving itself. That's kind of the essence of Christmas, isn't it?"

"Getting presents?" Heather asked.

117

Ethan laughed. "That is nice when someone remembers you, but it's like your mom was saying about the spirit of Saint Nick. It's about giving."

"Like what we've been talking about at church?" Heather asked. "How the three wise guys gave baby Jesus those presents?"

"Wise men, honey," Olivia said with a chuckle. "And yes. They were celebrating his birth with gifts, because Jesus gave us the ultimate gift of his life and sacrifice."

Olivia could see the cogs of Heather's mind turning while she connected the final pieces of Christmas traditions together. When she was satisfied, she put her hands on the table and stood up. "I want to help other people feel happy at Christmas, then."

Olivia's heart swelled with pride, and her eyes misted with tears that seemed to be floating at the surface lately. "That's a wonderful goal."

"I can think of fifteen people at church who have hardly anything. They shouldn't be forgotten at Christmas because they're poor," Heather said.

"Who's poor?" Emma said, stretching her arms over her head and yawning as she shuffled into the kitchen. Tightening her robe around her waist, she sat down next to Heather and smiled sleepily at her.

"People I know at church," Heather said, brushing her hair behind her ears. "I want to be like Santa, and do something to make them know they are loved."

Emma picked up her bowl and helped herself to a scoop of oatmeal from the pot. "Santa would surely appreciate that kind of help."

Heather tilted her head at Emma and matter-of-factly said, "I already know Santa's not actually real, Emma."

Emma blinked at Heather's confession. "Well, then. That

explains why you were asking all those outlandish questions last night. You were trying to trip me up, weren't you? It would've been easier if you'd told me you already knew about Santa."

Heather shrugged. "It was more fun pretending I didn't know to get you to answer my questions."

"You little stinker!" Emma cried, tilting her head back and howling with laughter. "If Santa *was* real, you might've been put on his naughty list for a stunt like that. I mean, you were trying to get me to remember all his reindeers' names and what Mrs. Claus looked like and how he got down the chimney, being as fat as he is."

"I would have paid to see you try to answer," Ethan said.

Emma huffed at her brother. "I doubt you would've been able to do any better than I could."

"Probably not. But serves you right," said Ethan with a smirk. "Heather reminds me a lot of what you were like as a kid."

"Sweet and adorable?" Heather asked with a giggle.

"That, but a bit of a troublemaker, too," Ethan said.

The happy chatter of breakfast continued long after the last of the oatmeal had been eaten. Sitting back in her chair, Olivia quietly watched as Heather laughed with Ethan and Emma. Whenever they had guests at the bed and breakfast, the Holly Wreath Inn had the appearance of liveliness, but with Emma and Ethan, it was like having a family. A warm feeling filled Olivia, and she could have lived in that moment forever.

Twila let herself in the back door and stomped the snow off her feet onto the rug.

"Yoo-hoo! Anybody ready for church?" she said as she moseyed into the kitchen, wearing a festive green dress with lace around the hem.

"Church!" Olivia said, jumping out of her seat and

119

hurrying to gather the dirty dishes into the sink. "What time is it?"

Ethan leaned back in his seat to look at the oven. "Looks like it's nine-forty."

"Church starts in twenty minutes," Olivia said, drying her hands on her pajama pants.

Ethan got up and helped clear the table. "Couldn't we catch the later meeting?"

"Ten o'clock *is* the later meeting," Olivia said.

"Ah. I'll go get dressed then. Will slacks and a tie be alright?" Ethan asked.

"You're going to church?" Emma asked.

"Yeah. I was invited," Ethan said. "You want to come, too?"

"Maybe I do," Emma answered.

"Then let's go. I won't hesitate to leave you behind if you're too slow," Ethan teased.

Emma backhanded him in the stomach, and he pretended to be mortally wounded, making Heather giggle with glee. "I bet I can beat you even if I put on eyeliner."

"And what are you going to wear there?" Ethan asked. "Silk pajamas?"

"No," Emma said. "I bought this cute little shift dress when we were shopping for Olivia's and your date. Mine screams small town church dress."

"Then I suppose we'd better get ready," Ethan said.

Emma pushed past Ethan and skipped up the stairs two at a time and slammed her door shut.

"What'd I tell you about her competitive nature?" Ethan said.

"It's legendary," Olivia agreed. "Heather. Go get changed. Wear that pretty dress we found at the thrift store."

"The blue one?" Heather said as she skittered to her room.

"That's the one. Be ready in ten minutes or we're going to

be late getting there. And put on some tights. It's cold outside," Olivia said.

Heather grumbled about Olivia's insistence on tights but went obediently to her bedroom. Hurrying to wipe off the table so the oatmeal didn't dry on it while they were away, Ethan emptied the garbage and put in a new bag.

"You really don't have to," Olivia said as she stacked the bowls and spoons into the dishwasher.

"Then you're going to have to stop, too," Ethan said. "If it's that important to you that you come home to a clean kitchen, then I'm alright showing up to church late with you."

She rinsed out the dishcloth and draped it over the sink, touched that he wasn't hurrying her along even though it would affect his arrival time too. "You're right. I should go get ready, too."

Twila cackled from where she'd pulled out a chair at the table. "At least she listens to you. We're late every other week because she's busy mopping or washing windows so she can come home to an impeccably clean home."

"I don't like to be sitting still at church, I guess," Olivia said, her cheeks burning slightly with embarrassment. "There's always something else I could've been doing instead of waiting for service to start."

"Having a little quiet time to contemplate isn't a bad thing once in a while," Ethan said. "Church is probably the best place of all to get it."

Twila clapped her hands and pointed. "Thank you! I haven't been able to get that through to her yet."

Rolling her eyes, Olivia would've disagreed, but she knew Twila was right. "Way to gang up on me, guys."

"What are friends for?" Twila said, drumming her fingers on the table. "Now go get yourself ready, or I'm going to have to take you two in your pajamas, and as cozy as they might be, call me old fashioned, I think you should put on your Sunday best."

Ethan left, running up the stairs to his room, while Olivia turned for her bedroom. She quickly pulled on her favorite cotton dress and wriggled into the black tights and boots she'd worn the night before. Pairing it with a simple gold chain necklace and dangling earrings, her outfit wasn't exceptionally ornate, but it made her feel feminine and appropriate for church.

She swiped on mascara and ran a tube of rosy-colored lipstick on before pinning her hair into a bun at the nape of her neck. Satisfied she looked presentable, she grabbed her pea coat on the way out.

Ethan was leaning against the countertop in the kitchen, his hands tucked in his pockets. She stopped, caught off guard by how handsome he looked with his hair parted and his button up shirt rolled up to his elbows. The way his eyes widened appreciatively, Olivia figured she must not have looked half-bad herself.

"Where is everyone?" Olivia asked as she put on her coat and buttoned it, making sure to tuck her scarf down the front.

"I offered to drive again, so I sent them out to the car," he said. "I forgot my wallet though and had to run in to get it. Figured we could walk out together."

Ethan held out his hand, and Olivia walked over to join him. The whole thing with him felt surreal. After Thanksgiving, she'd been hoping Christmas would at the very least be bearable. Little could she have imagined that it would be unforgettable.

"We'd better get going. Twila's right that we're always scrambling in late. It's pretty embarrassing," Olivia said.

Ethan's eyes glimmered, and he pulled her around to him,

resting his hands on her waist. "Could I sneak in one more of those kisses we shared last night?"

Putting her hands around his neck, she weaved her fingers together and tilted her face up toward his. "I guess there's always time for one more kiss."

CHAPTER 11

The bells were ringing in the steeple as everyone poured out of the car and ran to the church. The ushers were closing the doors to go take their seats, and the rest of the stragglers were hurrying in. Ethan had a hold of Olivia's hand, and she kept pace with him. Not to be outdone, Heather sprinted ahead with Emma hot on her heels.

"First!" Heather cried triumphantly as her hand touched the door.

"Only because you aren't wearing heels," Emma said. "I about broke my ankle racing you."

Heather tugged at the door while eyeing Emma's impractical shoes. "It's not my fault you're wearing those things. I don't even think I could walk in them, they're so high."

"Well, excuse me, missy," Emma teased. "They're what I had in my suitcase. I didn't know what I was supposed to pack when I came to rescue my brother."

Olivia looked to him, and the collar of his shirt felt too snug. She asked, "Rescue him? What are you in need of rescuing from?"

Emma backpedaled, but the question had been planted in Olivia's mind. It wasn't that he didn't want Olivia to ask, but the way Olivia had fretted over how to break the news to Heather about Santa Claus, Ethan felt the same anxiety about revealing to Olivia just who he was. The timing would need to be right, and he wanted to present it in an it's-not-a-big-deal sort of way.

"He decided to take some personal time and wouldn't tell me where he was." Emma shrugged, waiting in the entryway between the outer and inner doors while they waited for Twila to catch up. "When I found him in the middle of a tiny town I could barely find on the map, I was a little worried."

"Understandably so," Olivia said. Looking back to Ethan, she asked. "Are you? In need of rescuing?"

"Aren't we all?" Ethan said. "I think I proved that point when I caught you after you tipped off the ladder, right?"

"You caught her when she fell?" Emma asked. "Aww, how romantic!"

"It was only because some drunk pigeons were on a crash course for me," Olivia said. "But thank you all the same. I'm glad you were there for me."

Ethan said. "There you go. Everybody needs a little rescuing."

"Let's get in there before they finish the opening hymn," Twila said, hoofing it into the small church.

They quietly followed after Twila, hanging their coats in the coat room and filing into the only pew that was still available, in the middle of the right side.

"This is better seating than we normally get," Twila whispered. "It is a bit squished though."

Heather giggled as they tried to find space for everyone, until Olivia touched her finger to her lips to quiet her. Ethan didn't mind the tight squeeze. Olivia's side was pressed against his, and she didn't shy away when he draped his arm across the back to accommodate his shoulders.

After an opening prayer, the choir sang a melodic version of *O Holy Night* that set the tone for the preacher's sermon. Ethan was content to listen, but Heather kept looking around, barely able to sit still.

During the intermediate hymn of *Away in a Manger* where the congregation was invited to stand and sing with the choir, Olivia leaned over to Heather and asked, "What's the matter? You're as jittery as if you ate a whole stocking of chocolate."

"I'm making a mental list," Heather whispered back.

"A list? Of what?" Olivia asked, her face creased with confusion.

"Of people who could use help," Heather said. "There are so many just in church that could use a special Christmas."

"Like who?" Ethan asked as he looked over the crowd.

Heather pointed to an older lady in a sweater. "Ms. Shaffer was telling mom her car needs new tires, and that family over there," Heather pointed to where three small children sat between their parents, "I noticed their boots have holes."

Heather pointed out five other people there she'd thought of, and listed a dozen more at school and around town who she could name off the top of her head who had a specific need.

"Oh, sweetie," Olivia said as her chin quivered. "You're so observant and kindhearted, but I don't know how we could possibly help all of them. Things are a bit...tight at home. Maybe you could send them all a card? Or we could go caroling to their houses?"

Heather's shoulders slumped, and a defeated look clouded her usually cheerful demeanor. "A card won't keep anyone's feet warm and dry."

A tear spilled over Olivia's eyelashes, and Emma reached into her purse, pulling out a package of tissues. "Maybe Ethan and I could help."

"Really? Can you?" Heather hopped in place, and Olivia had to tug on her sleeve to get her to sit down when the hymn finished.

"Your heart is in the right place, but even they don't have enough money to buy things for everyone in need in Holly Wreath," Olivia whispered.

Ethan's heart beat faster as an idea popped into his head. "Actually, Emma's right. We might be able to help."

Olivia's eyebrows dipped lower, and she leaned in closer. "How?"

Ethan said, pushing aside her hair and stooping down to whisper in her ear, "Remember that charity I was telling you about?"

"Yeah…" she breathed.

Emma interrupted, reaching across Olivia to poke Ethan in the leg. "Do you know those girls?"

Across the room, five twenty-something-year-old girls were talking excitedly in hushed tones behind their hands and clearly looking in Ethan's direction.

"No. Why would I?" he asked, feeling an uncomfortable heat creeping up his neck. He didn't like the thought of attention being on him, especially from people he didn't know.

"They're looking at you like you're the last cookie on the plate," Emma said. "Do you know who they are, Olivia?"

"Not very well. They're here most weeks, but we don't really run in the same circles," Olivia answered. "They're probably staring because we keep talking while we're supposed to be listening to the sermon."

"Right," Ethan said, pinching his lips shut.

The rest of the hour, Ethan tried to focus on the words

127

the preacher shared from the pulpit. He caught bits of the message spoken about the miraculous birth of the Savior, and what could be done to share that message of love and hope, but he was too distracted to listen intently. Even more than the pew of girls continuing to stare and giggle, Olivia had taken his hand and was stroking his knuckles with her thumb. It was enough to drive him wild.

"That was a nice service," Twila said as they left the sanctuary and entered into a large room where donuts and orange juice had been set out while people socialized. "I always feel determined to be a new woman by the end of church."

"I know what you mean," Olivia said, sighing happily. Squeezing Ethan's hand, she said, "Thanks for coming with us today. It made it extra special."

"Happy to. I can't remember the last time I was able to go to church," Ethan said.

"You make time for what matters," Twila said, shaking a pointer finger at him and holding a powdered donut in the other hand, sprinkling sugar all over her dress.

Ethan let his head fall, and he rubbed the back of his neck. "You're right. I've been busy. I let myself get too busy."

"I can attest to that. He's a total stick-in-the-mud workaholic," Emma said.

Nudging him with her hip, Olivia said, "I've sure appreciated his work ethic while he's been here. We've almost finished the guest bedroom months before I anticipated it being done."

"It helps that I can hammer in a nail now without smashing my own fingers," Ethan joked.

"That definitely is a good thing. You're lucky you didn't lose a fingernail," Olivia said. "Maybe I'll teach you how to run the saw this week."

"Think I'm ready?" Ethan asked.

Olivia shrugged. "Guess we'll see if we end up in the emergency room."

They mingled for half an hour after church, enjoying the fresh donuts, and Olivia graciously accepted praise from a few of her fellow churchgoers who'd seen her play at the Christmas tree lighting. Heather was busy showing off the manicure she'd done with Emma the night before, while Emma and Twila bantered about who sang the best version of *The First Noel*.

"So," Heather said, finishing off a jelly-filled donut and licking her fingers, "I haven't forgotten about what you said in there. About your charity helping."

"Neither have I. I think it's very noble of you to want to help others in need," Ethan said. Lowering his voice so Olivia wouldn't hear from where she was standing at the water cooler speaking to the pastor, Ethan said, "I want you to make a list of everyone and what you think they could use to brighten their Christmas. I'll take care of the rest."

"The rest of what?" Olivia said as she sauntered back over. The smile on her face was teasing yet sweet, and Ethan wanted nothing more than to take her into his arms and hold her close.

"We were talking about how we could provide a little bit extra to those in need," Heather said.

"Heather," Olivia said in a warning tone. "I don't want you begging Ethan and Emma to help you out. It's such short notice and—"

"I don't think you understand," Emma said as she rejoined their circle. "Our charity has generous funds at its disposal. It isn't like we're digging change out of our own pockets to help Heather out."

"But I would if that's what was needed," Ethan said.

"See, Mom? They're willing to help. Please let me. It's like you said. If I know that Santa isn't the one delivering my gifts, I can play the part and give that happiness to others."

"Wait a minute," Twila said, pointing her finger between Heather and Olivia. "She doesn't…?"

Olivia shook her head. "Nope. She apparently already knew."

"Huh. Well, aren't you all grown up little lady?" Twila said.

"I'm practically ready to drive," Heather said, putting her hands on her hips.

"Just because you know the truth about Santa doesn't mean you should rush your way out of childhood," Olivia said.

"I won't," Heather promised. "I'm perfectly happy to let you keep doing my laundry for me."

"About that…I think it's about time for you to at least start folding it on your own," Olivia said, raising her brow.

Heather grumbled all the way to the coat closet, where Ethan handed out coats and helped Olivia put hers on. On their way to the door, Heather jumped unexpectedly, like she'd stepped on a tack.

"What?" Olivia asked.

"I had an idea," Heather said, a pleased look on her face.

When she didn't answer, Olivia coaxed, "Care to share it?"

Heather swung her arms while she spoke. "I was thinking that while I'm busy figuring out how to help a few people in Holly Wreath, maybe there's something we can do for you, Mom."

Warily, Olivia asked, "What are you thinking?"

"The inn. You're so close to finishing it, but I've heard you say more than once that if you just got a new roof on it, you'd be able to get the rest done, no problem. It's the roof that costs so much, and you haven't found out a way to pay for it," Heather said.

Olivia blushed red, and she looked down at her shoes. "That's true. It'll take quite a bit of work and time and money to get the roof taken care of, but I most certainly do not want Ethan paying for it."

Ethan eagerly stepped forward. Heather's suggestion was the perfect gesture of his admiration and budding love for Olivia, and though it wouldn't be cheap, it certainly wasn't the most expensive gift he'd ever given to a woman. The Corvette Mallory sped around Seattle in was evidence of that. "Are you sure? I'd be happy to—"

Holding up her hand to cut him off, Olivia said, "I appreciate the sentiment, I really do. But I'm going to have to have you promise me right here, right now, that you won't use your money or your charity's funds to get a new roof on my house. Call it a matter of pride, but I'm not looking for a handout."

Emma and Ethan exchanged a glance and both of them frowned. "Alright," Ethan said, tucking his hands into his suit and exhaling long and fast, "if that's what you wish. I won't contribute monetarily to getting a new roof on your home."

Satisfied, Olivia nodded, then stood on her tiptoes to give Ethan a quick kiss on the cheek. "Thanks."

With the rest of the patrons leaving to go home for lunch, Ethan offered to run out to the car. "Let me warm it up for a few minutes."

"No complaints from these old bones," Twila said, settling herself onto a floral couch. Heather plopped down next to Twila and pulled Emma down with her.

"That'd be nice. Appreciate it," Olivia said, giving his hand one more squeeze before she started helping gather the scattered trash from around the room and dumping it into a rolling garbage can.

The cold seemed to steal the breath right out of his lungs, and the sun gave a false sense of hope that it would do anything to warm the day. He jogged cautiously over to the car and pulled out the keys, watching out for any patches of ice. Near his rental, another car approached slowly. He thought nothing of it until it pulled to a stop a few feet away from him.

One of the girls that had been whispering and gawking the entire service leaned out of the window, giving him a dazzling smile. "You're Ethan Wilder, aren't you?"

Ethan's insides felt like a balloon that had been pricked with a tack. In the back of his mind, he'd known it was only a matter of time before he was discovered. It was the nature of his existence, and he'd enjoyed his run at living a semi-normal life in an unpresumptuous small town. Even then, news and the internet made the whole world a smaller place.

He thought momentarily about denying it, but lying felt wrong, especially after attending church. "I am."

"I knew it!" she squealed, and the rest of the girls whooped and giggled along with her. "We weren't sure, especially since you're here in Holly Wreath of all places, but I just knew. They had a spread about you in a magazine I was reading at my hairdresser's."

"How nice," Ethan said, wondering how he could get through the surprise meet and greet that had been sprung on him. "If you'll excuse me, I've got to—"

"You're a lot more handsome in person," said the blond in the passenger seat. "Every time I see a photo of you, you've got the smolder going."

Ethan opened the driver's side door and leaned over the hood. "The paparazzi doesn't exactly give their subjects a heads up."

Ethan tried to excuse himself again, but a redhead with freckles on every inch of her body rolled down the window behind the driver and blurted, "So sorry to hear about your engagement to Mallory. I was sure you two were a match made in heaven. Your wedding was going to be like the marriage of American royalty."

Ethan had to suppress an eyeroll. "Yes, well. It's probably all for the best."

"Can I have an autograph?" asked a third girl, who wore thick-glasses that made her look like a librarian. She reached around the redhead and waved a napkin and pen.

Ethan kept his smile in place, though it was beginning to feel strained. As far as fans went, they were tame enough. "Of course."

One autograph led to half a dozen more as the girls combed the car for every scrap of paper they could find. When they ran out, they exited the car with phones in hand.

"Can we take some selfies?" The driver asked, smacking on her gum and twirling her brunette hair while she eagerly anticipated his response. She wasn't going to take no for an answer.

"Everybody lean in," Ethan said, trying desperately to be patient.

"Say cheese!" said the redhead.

Forcing another smile at the center of the group, a nagging thought settled at the back of his mind.

I hope I don't regret this.

CHAPTER 12

"Operation Secret Santa has officially commenced!" Heather said gleefully.

They were in the front living room, and every inch of furniture and tables were covered in gifts, as was most of the floor. Heather had spent the rest of Sunday curled up on the couch with a notepad on her lap, thinking of everyone she possibly could who could use some Christmas cheer. When Olivia had tried to rein her in, Ethan and Emma dismissed Olivia, reassuring her the charity would take care of it.

"Just how big is your charity?" she'd asked, realizing her question was a bit nosy.

Ethan had grinned boyishly and answered proudly, "Big enough."

Olivia had made her usual Sunday dinner of pot roast and rolls, with a chocolate mousse pie to send Emma back to Seattle on a full stomach. When Heather began to cry about Emma's imminent departure, tears filmed Emma's eyes, too. She promised she'd be back as soon as she could, saying she needed to bring Rob to meet everyone.

Before Ethan took her to the local airport where their company's jet was waiting to take her back, Emma had given Olivia a tight hug and whispered into her ear, "Thank you for being so wonderful to Ethan. He's the happiest I've ever seen him when he's with you."

The compliment had made Olivia's heart soar, and for the first time in a long time, she'd let herself get her hopes up.

Standing near the fireplace with a stack of shoeboxes at her feet, Twila clapped her hands. "Alright. These presents aren't going to wrap themselves. Turn on the Christmas music, Olivia. We've got our work cut out for us."

"I can't believe you've bought all of this," Olivia said, turning a slow circle.

"I'd be happy not to have to go shopping again for a very long time. I literally have spent over twenty-four hours shopping the past three days alone, and that's not including what I did online," Ethan said. "I think props really have to go to Heather for coming up with this plan and figuring out all the little details."

Heather came in with an armful of wrapping paper, tape, and scissors. "Twila helped me with the small stuff, like figuring out clothing sizes and favorite colors and stuff."

"All that chit chat I do with people around town really paid off," Twila said.

Heather put down the supplies and held her hands out, showing Olivia her accomplishment. "Now that you've seen how much I can get done when I'm not at school, can I stay home the rest of the week?"

Olivia chuckled. "I will give you that I am impressed, but after we get these wrapped tonight, you're going back to school at least for Thursday so you can pick up the homework you've missed. We're not delivering them until Friday, before Ethan leaves Saturday."

The words slipped out of her mouth without much

thought, until it dawned on her that Ethan's reservation was over in less than four days, and that made the whole room somber. Olivia knew it was coming, but it still stung. Their relationship was still blossoming, but she'd fallen hard and fast for him. Still, she had tried desperately to squash any daydreaming about what the future might hold for them.

Trying to change the mood, Olivia turned on a Christmas radio station and asked, "Who's got the list?"

Ethan held up a stack of papers stapled together. "I do. First on the list is the Hernandez family. They've got quite the haul, so we'd better get started."

For the next three hours, they cut and taped and wrapped presents, making sure to carefully label them and put them into organized piles, while Twila mapped out their route. She figured it was going to take at least twelve hours, planning for stops to eat and use the restroom, to deliver everything.

When they got to Ms. Shaffer and the four tires stacked in the corner of the entryway, Olivia said with a laugh, "I'm not going to be able to wrap those."

"No worries," Ethan said. He rummaged through the wrapping paper and bows he'd bought and pulled out a sparkly green bag, shaking it open to its full size. "I'm pretty sure this bag is big enough to fit a horse."

Olivia propped her hands on her hips, shaking her head in awe. "You really did think of everything, didn't you?"

Ethan's cheeks pinkened adorably, and he shrugged off her compliment. "It's kind of in my nature to be organized. Comes in handy at my job."

"Do you really have to go back to work?" Heather whined. "I like having you around."

Ethan laughed, rubbing his hand on Heather's head. Olivia focused on picking up pieces of spare wrapping paper that were too small to use for anything else and stuffed them into the already-full garbage. She had been thinking the same thing as Heather, though she'd never say it out loud. Being an adult sometimes was harder than she liked to admit.

"Unfortunately, yes," Ethan said. "I can do most of my job remotely, but sometimes, even I have to go into the office and do things in person."

Ethan glanced over at Olivia, and she tried to smile, but it was faint. The wave of sadness she felt was matched by Ethan, though it went unspoken. It was possible that he'd leave and never come back. She knew it was a possibility but hadn't prepared herself for it. While she indulged herself by living in the moment, she'd inadvertently become more attached to her future.

"I'll be back as soon as I can," Ethan promised. "I wouldn't want to miss Christmas this year."

"Changing your mind about things, are you?" Olivia said.

"About all sorts of things," Ethan said. Olivia grinned and said a silent prayer that this year, Christmas really would be different.

The next few days were bittersweet. Ethan assured her repeatedly his leaving wasn't going to be the last time she saw him, but the nagging worry in the back of her mind kept reminding her that once Jeff had left, he'd never returned. The thought made her sick to her stomach not only for herself but for Heather. She and Ethan had gotten along like they'd always known each other.

Olivia tried to keep herself busy between cooking and running the house, working on the guest bedroom, and doing her errands or practicing her violin when Ethan was on conference calls. When the paycheck from the diner arrived, she finished the last of her Christmas shopping, including a gift for Ethan which she'd added to her list. Things were already tight, but she forewent a few of the splurges on her grocery list, including new socks for herself.

It was Thursday afternoon when she was walking back to

her car in the Main Street district where she'd bought Twila a bag of boutique licorice when Olivia saw it. A small watercolor painting of the tree lighting in Holly Wreath sat in a window display. It wasn't much larger than a postcard, but it was in a rustic wooden frame and impeccably captured the warm glow of the Christmas tree's lights when it shone against the cold December evenings. It took less time for Olivia to deliberate about getting it for Ethan than she'd spent picking out candy for Twila.

At home, she set down her finds on the counter, and she took out the picture to admire it one more time. She almost wished there was a duplicate she could've hung in the inn, but Olivia wanted Ethan to have something to remind him of his time in Holly Wreath—of her. It was a small plea that she hoped would encourage him to come back to her.

Flipping over the picture, she found a silvery permanent marker in one of her drawers and scrawled a brief message, wishing him a Merry Christmas, and signing it *Love, Olivia*.

The back door opened and shut. Twila called, "Olivia? You back yet?"

"In here!" Olivia called.

Realizing she had Twila's gift laying on the island, she hurriedly stashed it in a cabinet with the mixing bowls. Twila strolled in, wearing only a sweater over a turtleneck, no coat.

"It's like a heatwave outside," Twila said, fanning herself and pushing her sleeves up to her elbows.

"I know. The weatherman said it's going to be fifty tomorrow. At the rate we're going, we might not have snow for Christmas."

Twila sat down on a stool and leaned against the island countertop. "I'm sure the cold will find us again. I'm going to take any mild winter days that I can get."

"It's still technically autumn," Olivia teased.

Rolling her eyes and groaning, Twila said, "Don't remind

me. Once New Year's Day is over, I'm done with the snow. Maybe I should become a snowbird and fly down to Corpus Christi when my joints start to ache from the cold."

"Then who would keep me company?"

"I think Ethan would happily do it. And don't you try to pretend you don't think the same thing, too." Twila's eyes sparkled, and though Olivia tried to be modest, her face turned crimson, and she sputtered a laugh.

"It would be nice, yes. But we've only been on one actual date, and the rest has been spent hanging out and working on the house and spending time with Heather."

"So it sounds like you've been spending plenty of time together," Twila said. "Sort of like a family does."

Olivia laughed softly while she emptied the contents of the rest of her bags. "I think you're jumping the gun a bit on that one."

"I know I am, but in case you've forgotten, I'm older and wiser than both of you combined, and I know what's most important in life. I see how happy you are with him and how he pushes you just enough to stretch you out of your comfort zone, while you help him learn to relax and that he doesn't have to be so serious all the time. I don't know what the future holds for the two of you, but enjoy the here and now, and don't be afraid to give your heart to someone else. You of all people deserve that happiness."

Olivia tucked her chin into her chest, afraid Twila might catch her crying, but it was helpless to try and hide anything from her. Twila patted her on the cheek, and Olivia sniffled. "Sorry for getting all weepy. I think that's what I wanted to hear. I have this underlying fear that we're too different from each other to really make it work."

"Sometimes, I think it's those differences that keep a couple balanced. I know it certainly kept my marriage interesting, and I loved my husband all the more for it. For you,

I'd love nothing more than to see you get your own Merry Christmas with Ethan," Twila said. Spotting the watercolor on the table, she picked it up to admire it. "Is this for him?"

Olivia nodded, soaking up the rest of her tears with the hem of her t-shirt. "I'm lousy at figuring out gifts for people, but I wanted to send him off with something so he'd remember me when he's back in Seattle."

"I think it's perfect. It gives me the warm fuzzies inside."

"Good," Olivia said. "I think I'm going to sneak it into his suitcase so he doesn't find it until he gets home. He should have his own little surprise, especially since he's been such a help making this Christmas extra special for so many people in Holly Wreath."

"Agreed. Between him and Heather, I thought they were going to clear out everything at the stores. It was very generous of him, and your girl is something special. It's been a lot of fun seeing her with a man like Ethan. That's the kind of father figure she deserves in her life."

"They really are great together," Olivia murmured, losing herself in a fantasy about being a complete family again.

"Well," Twila said drumming her hands on the countertop, "I came over to see if I could be of any help before we get everything packed up and send you off to complete your Christmas mission, delivering presents all day tomorrow. Would it help if I went to pick up Heather from school?"

"Actually, that'd be great. I can get a jumpstart on dinner."

Twila craned her neck and looked out the window above the kitchen sink. "And maybe get in a few kisses with Ethan without interruption?"

"Twila!" Olivia said, her face growing warm. "I can't believe you."

"What? You think because I have gray hairs I don't know what it's like to be young and in love?"

Grinning, Olivia shook her head as she pulled out her

griddle to make French toast and bacon for dinner. "If you must know, Ethan is an excellent kisser, and I wouldn't complain one bit about getting another from him."

"I guess that answers my question then. I'll go pick up Heather. You want me to take the scenic route home?"

"Twila!" Olivia said, using her spatula to shoo her out the door.

Ethan opened the back door to let himself in as Twila left, laughing so hard she couldn't even greet him properly. Giving her a strange look, Ethan shut the door behind him and asked, "What was that all about?"

"It's…Twila. What else can I say?" Olivia said as she rummaged through the meat drawer for the hickory smoked bacon.

"Ah. No need to explain," Ethan said. "She reminds me very much of a fun great aunt I had. Always up to something."

He leaned against the wall and put one foot up, hooking his thumbs in his belt loops. His handsomeness didn't escape Olivia's notice. She knew she was lucky he'd set his sights on her when he could probably make any woman within a five mile radius swoon with just a smile.

"So. What've you been up to today? Out saving the world?" Olivia asked. She carefully set the bacon on the hot griddle where it hissed and sizzled.

"Not exactly the whole world, but a small piece of it nonetheless. I was tying up a few loose ends in town before I have to go back to Seattle."

"I see," Olivia said, forcing down the lump in her throat.

She was glad her back was to him and that the sound of bacon frying covered up another sniffle. Her emotions were swarming at the surface, and it felt like the smallest thing might tip her into a sobbing mess.

Behind her, she could sense Ethan's gaze in her direction,

but she pretended to be ignorant of where his gorgeous hazel eyes were focused. Without a word, he crossed the room and took the spatula out of her hand, setting it on the counter. Putting his hands on her hips, he spun her around to face him.

"I'm going to miss you, you know," he said in a low, husky voice.

Olivia swallowed as she watched his mouth say the words. "I understand, though. You have a life outside of this little inn."

"Yeah, but I'm envisioning a new trajectory for my life. One with you in it."

Olivia's heart fluttered in her chest. That was the kind of affirmation she wanted from him. "I'd like that."

Ethan pulled her in closer and started a list. "You, me, Heather, Christmas morning, your hot chocolate, a roaring fire, and Frank Sinatra singing Christmas music. What do you think?"

Olivia pressed her lips to his, enjoying his closeness until they both were breathless, with hearts racing. "That sounds like my kind of Christmas morning."

CHAPTER 13

Ethan was up by five in the morning and was on the rug by the end of the bed, doing push-ups to burn off the excess energy that was making him jittery and excited. He was going to spend the whole day with Olivia and Heather delivering presents to people all over Holly Wreath. What was making him most excited was the surprise he had planned for Olivia. The sooner he could get her out the door the better.

He showered and put on a pair of jeans and a t-shirt he'd gotten from participating in a half marathon down in Portland a few years back. Cracking open his door, he held his breath and listened. In the dark, the gentle strains of violin music filtered through the silence. He smiled. Olivia must have been as excited as he was if she was up early, playing her violin. One thing he knew about Olivia Campbell was that she was *not* a morning person if she could help it, so if she was up, something was on her mind.

Deciding it was safe to leave his room, he went quietly, wincing each time the stairs creaked. Two steps down, he swung his leg over the banister like he'd seen Heather do on countless occasions and slid to the bottom. His prim and proper grandparents had never let him do it on their stairs, and despite being a grown man, the act made him feel like a carefree child.

To help the morning move along, Ethan was going to get a light breakfast together, then get Olivia and Heather into the truck he'd rented and they'd stuffed with gifts. There was so much to do, but he was eager to rise to the challenge.

He entered the kitchen at the same time as Olivia, and he flipped on the lights so he could better see her. "You couldn't sleep either, huh?"

Twisting her damp hair into a bun and securing it with a hair tie, Ethan could see the excitement lighting her eyes. "Nope. I honestly haven't been this giddy about Christmas presents since I was a little girl, and I'm not even the one getting them," she said.

"That's what I admire so much about you," Ethan said.

Tipping her head to the side, she asked, "What?"

Ethan took two long strides and wrapped his arms around Olivia, drawing her close. He tucked her hair behind her ear for her, and she grinned. Life was complete with Olivia. "You're excited for other people, probably even more than you are for yourself."

Smiling, Olivia elevated herself on her toes to give him a kiss, though it was cut short by Heather clapping.

"Alright, break it up," Heather said, standing in the doorway and puffing her chest out authoritatively. "We haven't got time for all this lovey dovey mushy stuff today. We've got to get on the road."

"Breakfast first," Olivia said. "It's going to be a long day."

Ethan helped Olivia get together a quick but hearty breakfast, and they were out the door. Counting it as a win in his book, Ethan had even managed to convince Olivia to leave the dirty dishes in the sink, reassuring her they'd be there when they got back.

"It almost feels like spring out here," Olivia said as she locked the back door.

"Well, I want a white Christmas. It doesn't seem right without it," Heather said.

"When you figure out how to get the weather to do what you want, let me know," Olivia said, laughing at her daughter.

Olivia unlocked the garage and pulled open the door where they'd parked the truck. Olivia ran her fingertips across the shiny chrome grill. "This sure is a beautiful truck. Too bad it's only a rental."

"Maybe I'll buy you one. Think it'll fit under the tree?" Ethan quipped.

Olivia blinked at his comment. "Just how much money do you have?"

Ethan couldn't look her in the eyes as his face flushed. "Sorry. Bad joke."

"Too bad. I'd like to ride around in a truck like this," Heather said as she hopped in the back seat and slid to the middle, bouncing on the seat to test how comfy it was.

Olivia shook her head and rubbed her hand across her forehead. "I'm sorry. That was totally out of line. Your finances are none of my business."

He debated if now was the time to tell her who he was, but he couldn't bring himself to do it. He'd seen too many relationships in his life sour because of money. *His* money. What he had with Olivia was too special to screw it up by sharing what was in his bank account. If nothing else, it could wait until they were unwinding on the couch when the day was done.

"Water under the bridge," Ethan said, climbing into the driver's seat and starting up the truck. Driving slowly out with their cargo, Heather leaned forward from the back and smacked him on the arm.

"Aren't you forgetting something?" Heather gave him a very obvious, pointed look that Olivia only missed because she was perusing over the list.

"Right. Whoops," Ethan said climbing out of the truck.

"What are you doing?" Olivia asked. "Did we forget something?"

"Just wanted to double check that it's all strapped in. It'd be a shame to have presents falling out at every turn," Ethan said. "Hang on a sec."

Ethan jogged to the back of the truck, pretending to fumble with the tow straps but pulling out his phone to send Twila the signal that they were leaving. The lights at Twila's house across the street snapped on immediately after.

"Huh," Olivia said as he climbed back into the truck. "Twila's up early today. She must not've been able to sleep."

Ethan put the truck into gear. "She doesn't normally wake up now?"

"It's six in the morning," Olivia said as she rifled through her purse for some lip balm. "Nobody purposefully wakes up this early unless they have to. When we get back, I'm going to fall asleep before I hit the sack."

A grin tugged at Ethan's mouth, and he looked sideways at Olivia. "Hit the sack?"

"Yeah. You know. Laying your head down on the pillow. Jumping in bed," Olivia expounded.

Heather leaned between them. "It's Mom's weird Southern heritage. I don't know what she's saying half the time either."

"I've heard it a time or two myself," Ethan teased.

"Sorry, I can't help myself sometimes," Olivia said, laughing.

Taking her hand, Ethan brought it to his mouth and kissed her knuckles. "No need to apologize. I think it's cute."

He loved the way Olivia blushed and pushed her hair behind her ear while she tried to get herself under control.

"Alright," Heather said as she clapped. "Eyes on the road. We need to get to work if we're going to be able to be Santa for a day."

"Yes, ma'am," Ethan drawled.

Crinkling her nose at him, Olivia said, "That's your impression of a southern accent?"

"Yeah. Why?" he asked.

"Because you sounded like a Jamaican," Olivia said, pressing her fingers to her mouth, trying to hold back stammering laughter threatening to break out of her.

"One accent is the same as the next, right?" Ethan said, laughing himself.

"Not even close," Heather said with a repulsed expression. "You're really need to work on your impersonations. They're not very good."

Ethan caught Olivia's gaze, and the giggle she'd been suppressing came ripping out of her. Everyone in the car succumbed, howling for several blocks, unable to stop themselves. While they tried to regain their composure, Ethan couldn't help but think that there, in the truck, laughing and out doing early morning service with Olivia's hand in his, he couldn't remember a time when he was happier.

"Oh, there's the first house," Olivia said, perking up in her seat. "It's Mr. Kip."

Heather held the master list and scanned down it for his name. "One food basket and a comfy new blanket for him!"

Ethan pulled the car down an out-of-sight alleyway and looked at Olivia. "You want to do the honors?"

"Like, sneak his gifts on his porch, ring his doorbell, and run?"

147

"That's the general idea, yeah."

"Alright. Wish me luck," Olivia said as she opened her door and slipped out of the truck.

She rummaged through the back and found Mr. Kip's items, then headed in the direction of his modest gray bungalow. The minutes ticked by, and Ethan watched in his rearview mirror, his leg jiggling nervously while they waited. He'd been part of companywide fundraisers and given keynote speeches at charity events, but something about going out and doing the hands-on volunteer work was so much more exhilarating and fulfilling.

"What's taking her so long?" Heather asked, her own fingers fidgeting anxiously.

"I'm not sure. You want to jump out and see if—"

Olivia came tearing around the corner, a wide smile on her face. She opened the passenger door of the truck and squealed as she got in as if Mr. Kip was hot on her heels.

"Did he see you?" Heather asked, bouncing up and down in her seat.

"Nope. I rang the doorbell and hid behind his porch column," she said while she buckled herself.

"What took you so long then?" Heather asked.

"I wanted to stay and see his reaction. That's part of the fun of fulfilling the role of Santa. Seeing the happiness on another person's face is the best reward."

Ethan took Olivia's hand again. "Did he like it?"

"I think so. He was laughing and crying at the same time. I'd consider that a win."

Heather clapped her hands, her pent up energy and excitement threatening to boil over. "This is so much fun! Let's go do the next people!"

House after house, they delivered gifts, taking turns to be the one who rang the doorbell and ran. There were a few close calls where the people heard them struggling to carry the gifts to the front door, but each time they managed to scramble out of sight before being spotted.

"Did you see the look on Ms. Shaffer's face?" Heather said, sitting back in her seat and sipping on the soda that had come with her kid's meal. "I thought her face might crack if she smiled any wider."

"I can imagine it came as a big surprise, having a stack of new tires in a bag mysteriously delivered on your front porch," Olivia said. "I'm sure that's a weight off her mind knowing she doesn't have to figure out how to pay for those."

"I almost felt bad when she started crying," Heather said. Rummaging through her bag, she pulled out her last chicken nugget and dunked it in the ranch.

"Well, happiness at that level makes a person do all kinds of funny things," Olivia said. "I think ninety percent of the people we've seen today have cried."

Ethan knew the feeling. He could have scarcely imagined all that awaited him when he'd rolled into Holly Wreath a few weeks earlier, but in that short time, he'd been reminded of what was most important and been lucky enough to find it. Having admitted to himself that he loved Olivia, it felt like she'd always been a natural part of his life.

Now he needed to find the courage to say it out loud to her.

The three of them finished dinner on the drive to the handful of remaining stops they had. So far, everything had gone off without a hitch—the right presents made it to the right houses, they managed to remain anonymous, and everyone was overjoyed at the welcome surprise they found on their porches.

After delivering a large bag of dog food and a new dog bed to Heather's music teacher who was fresh out of college and still living humbly, then a new set of knitting needles and several skeins of yarn to an older woman at church who knitted items to sell at the local farmer's market to supplement her income, they arrived at their last stop.

"I think we're all going to have to carry things over for this one," Ethan said. "They got a lot of stuff."

Olivia sipped her soda and shook the cup to see if it was empty. With only ice left, she peeled back the lid and tipped her cup to get a mouthful, munching lightly on the ice. "Pass me the list, would you Heather?"

"Who's the lucky last person?" Ethan asked.

"Not one. Five. It's the Hernandez family," Olivia said, double checking the master list to make sure everyone else had gotten their gifts.

"Oh, yay!" Heather said, balling up her fists and shaking them with excitement. "I've been waiting to deliver their stuff all day. Their kids are going to be so excited!"

"We'd better get to it, then. I'm not sure what time the kids go to bed, but it's already seven thirty," Olivia said.

"I call ringing the doorbell," Heather said as she slid out of the truck and ran to the back to grab two of the four bags full of presents.

The three of them crept quietly up the Hernandez's porch to unload the gifts, placing them in a neat arrangement in front of the door. Through a window, a small Christmas tree sparkled with blue and white lights. There were a few handmade ornaments hanging from the branches, and from somewhere in the home, Ethan could hear laughter.

"Ready?" Heather whispered, her finger hovering over their doorbell.

"Where are we going to hide?" Olivia asked. "I want to see the surprise on their faces."

Ethan had noticed a small unkempt line of hedges between their home and an abandoned house that had been boarded up next door. Pointing to it, he said, "I think that'll hide us well enough."

"I'm getting a head start," Olivia said in hushed tones. "My feet are so tired that I'm not sure I'm going to be able to run another step."

"You got it, Heather?" Ethan asked. "I'm going to carry your mom over to our hiding spot."

"Carry me?" Olivia said, shaking her head. "Oh, no, you're not."

Ethan moved a step closer with his hands out, ready to spring. Olivia let out a squeal and slapped her hand over her mouth to keep from ruining their secretive operation. Bounding off the steps, she giggled uncontrollably as she sprinted. Ethan was hot on her heels, laughing himself as he closed the gap. He reached out and grabbed her wrist, slowing her enough that he scooped her up in his arms. He jogged the rest of the way to the bushes and clutched her to his chest.

"When I say I'm going to do something, I mean it," Ethan said as his heart raced.

"I didn't actually need you to carry me over here, but I guess thank you," Olivia said, putting her hands around the back of his neck. "I can't remember the last time I was swept off my feet."

"You deserve to be once in a while," Ethan said in a low voice.

Leaning in close, Olivia pressed her mouth on his, her kiss sweet but full of desire and longing. Pulling away, she let out a sigh as he trailed his lips down her cheek and jawline, then nuzzled his face into the crook of her neck. "If it's you doing the wooing me off my feet, I'm more than okay with it."

"Good," Ethan said, stealing another kiss.

From the porch, Heather hissed, "I'm ringing it. Are you guys ready?"

"Yes!" they whispered in unison.

Ethan put Olivia back on her feet, though he stayed close to her. She parted the branches of the untamed yew bush so they could get a clearer view, and Ethan watched from over her shoulder. Heather rang the doorbell several times, then jumped off the porch, letting out a high-pitched shriek of excitement. She rounded the corner of the yard to their hiding spot, panting and sliding to a stop as the Hernandez's porch light turned on, and the door swung open.

Their three small children peered out from behind their mother's legs, and when they realized the porch was covered with presents, they couldn't contain their exhilaration and ran out in their pajamas to look at them.

"Aww, look how happy Cici is! And Marco is going to shake that box until the toy inside is in pieces," Heather said as she giggled uncontrollably, wrapped up in watching their delight unfold.

Olivia shushed Heather so they wouldn't be spotted, but Ethan was busy watching their mother. She stood stone still, her hands covering her open mouth, and her eyes were wide and glassy as she absorbed everything in front of her.

"Do you think she's alright?" Ethan whispered to Olivia.

Olivia turned her head slightly, and Ethan noted her lips were only a few inches from his. "Maria? I think so. It looks like she's just surprised. I know I would be."

The three of them watched for a few moments longer, then Heather tapped on Ethan's arm and tossed her head toward the truck and winked. "Think we should get going?"

Ethan turned his wrist to see his watch in the brilliant, silvery moonlight that shone from overhead. "Yeah, we probably should go."

Olivia's bunched her eyebrows, and Ethan knew he was being too conspicuous. "In a hurry to get somewhere?"

"No. I'm just tired," Heather said straight-faced. Whether

it was true or not, it saved Ethan from having to cover his tracks.

"Let's go then," Olivia said, turning back to where they'd parked. "I'm pretty worn thin myself."

"Wait!" Heather hissed urgently and grabbing her mother's wrist. "Look!"

Maria was down on her knees. Ethan was about to run over to help her when he realized she wasn't slumped down, threatening to pass out, but she was about to pray.

Maria wiped tears from her cheeks and waved her hands at her children, gathering them over to her.

"We must pray. Kneel down so we can thank the Lord for the kind hands who have blessed us with these gifts," Maria said.

In a quiet voice, Maria said a heartfelt prayer, and as Ethan strained to hear, he could pick up bits and pieces of what she was saying. She thanked God for the beautiful day they'd been given, for the night job her husband was sacrificing to be at so they could have a roof over their head and food on their table. With more tears streaming down her face, she thanked God for the gifts.

She sniffled and wiped away her tears. "Please pour out blessings on those angels who have been so kind and generous in remembering our family this Christmas season. Help them know of our gratitude. They are the kind of people who brighten this world and make it a better place."

Next to him, Olivia put face into her hands, and her shoulders shook as she quietly sobbed. Ethan rubbed his hand on her back, and Heather, grinning at her mother's emotional reaction, hugged her. When Maria finished and gave each one of her children a kiss on the cheek and directed them to take the gifts inside and put them under the tree, she followed them inside. She looked around one last time into the darkness, looking for any sign of whomever had dropped off the gifts before she retreated inside and turned off the porch light.

The ride back to Holly Wreath Inn was quiet, as each of them contemplated what they'd accomplished that day. Ethan had rarely felt so satisfied with a day's work, and for the first time in a long time, he knew he'd directly made a difference in someone else's life. Thinking of the surprise he had waiting back at Olivia's house, he pressed his foot harder on the gas pedal.

"Today was wonderful," Olivia said. She rested her head against the seat and watched the world passing by, her voice dreamy and content. "Even though I'm exhausted, hungry, and can hardly keep my eyes open, I don't think I could've imagined a better way to celebrate Christmas than by serving others. Thank you, you two, for making it possible."

"You were a big help, too, Mom," Heather said. "I think you probably wrapped half the presents singlehandedly."

Olivia chuckled softly. "Glad I could do something to be useful."

Ethan's phone buzzed in his pocket, and he pulled it out to glance at it. Twila had sent him a message that everything was all finished, and they were scurrying to put everything back the way they had found it. A dose of adrenaline rushed through Ethan's veins. It was almost time to give the best gift of all—the one he'd arranged for Olivia.

"Hey. No texting and driving," Olivia said, holding out her hand. "Hand over the phone, mister."

Ethan fumbled with his phone and stuck it back in his coat pocket so Olivia wouldn't spoil the secret by seeing Twila's message. "You're right. I shouldn't be a distracted driver. I was, uh, waiting on something from Emma. You know. Work stuff."

"Even your sister can wait," Olivia said, taking his hand in hers.

Olivia turned on the radio, and the rest of the drive home, they sang along karaoke-style to the music. The instant they rounded the corner to Olivia's house, Olivia went silent. She sat up in her seat, and confusion overtook her as she stared at her home.

"Why are there so many cars in front of the inn? And why is there a dumpster parked in the driveway?" she asked.

Ethan pulled up the driveway, where a group of people were standing on the lawn, eagerly awaiting the moment they'd been anticipating all day.

"They're here helping me with something," Ethan said. "Working on a gift for you, actually. Merry early Christmas, Olivia."

CHAPTER 14

"For me?" Olivia said. Understanding dawned over her as she put it all together. There were ladders and scaffolding all around the house, a few people were hanging the Christmas lights back on the gutters, and the dumpster was full of old discarded shingles. Olivia shook her head and her eyes grew wide with panic. "No. You didn't."

"Isn't it incredible, Mom?" Heather said, shaking her shoulders. "We got a new roof!"

Hot anger flashed through Olivia, and she tried to hold it back, but her words came out tersely. "You promised me you wouldn't."

Ethan reined in a smirk, trying to keep her from getting more upset. "I promised *I* wouldn't pay for a roof through my charity. I didn't drop a dime of my own money, if that makes you feel better. All I gave was my time."

The anger that was simmering dissipated and was replaced by tears that threatened to fall. "It's just, you shouldn't have. All of it could have been put to better use helping someone else."

Ethan let out a laugh. "Olivia, you have to be the most

self-sacrificing woman I know. You spent the last week planning and executing a massive secret Santa operation, and you're upset because you were on the receiving end of a gift from others?"

"We passed out dog food and kid's toys all day. A new roof is a major renovation! I can't imagine how much it all cost," Olivia said. Her throat felt like it was constricting, making it hard to breathe.

"Calm down, Mom. You're overreacting and blaming Ethan," Heather said, patting her mom on the back. "He wasn't the only one who helped arrange it. Twila and I helped Ethan by finding people who could help."

Olivia was still in shock and couldn't find the words to express the swirl of emotions that bombarded her. The generosity of the people smiling at her from her lawn, the enormity of the gift they'd given, and the love she felt from Ethan and Heather and Twila threatened to overwhelm her.

Ethan got out of the truck and ran around to Olivia's side to open the door for her. Heather jumped out and tugged on her mom's hands, encouraging her from the truck.

"I hope you like the shingles we picked," Ethan said. "Twila said you'd had your eye on them for a while."

"They're perfect. But they were so expensive. I know, because I'd gotten a quote on them last year and was trying to save up for them," Olivia said, wiping at her tears with the sleeve of her jacket.

Twila pulled Olivia into a hug, patting her on the back. "Don't you worry about cost, honey. For one, the inn really did need the roof. We found a couple of spots that were starting to rot. Got some new plywood on them, and the ceiling is as good as new. You'll be able to redo the attic room now, just like you always wanted."

Olivia shook her head again, and a smile broke out on her

face. "I still can't believe it. Thank you, everyone. I can't believe you pulled it off!"

"Mostly, anyway," Twila said. "The dumpster can't be picked up until Monday, but everything else should be done. The best part of this gift is that you don't have to lift a finger for it."

Tears accumulated in her eyes, and laughing while she cried, she buried her face into Ethan's chest. She relished the feel of his strong arms around her, and as happy as she'd been all day, the joy she experienced felt like it would make her burst at the seams.

Giving each person there a hug and her heartfelt thanks, one by one, people left to go back to their homes, leaving Twila, Ethan, Heather, and Olivia admiring the craftsmanship of the new roof.

"Well, I'm pooped," Twila said. "Thank you, Heather and Ethan, for letting me be a part of your covert operation. It won't be a feeling soon forgotten, especially since I'll be able to see that beautiful new roof out of my kitchen window!"

"Ah," Olivia said, shaking her pointer finger at Twila. "I get it now. That's who you were texting all day, wasn't it, Ethan? You weren't waiting on anything from Emma, were you?"

Ethan's mouth twitched into a one-sided grin. "Yes and no. Emma has been sending me some work stuff, but I was hiding behind that excuse to keep in touch with Twila so we didn't come back too soon."

"Well, good job. I'm still in shock," Olivia said.

"I'm going to have a cup of cinnamon tea, read one chapter in my book, and will probably fall asleep before my head hits the pillow." Twila gave Olivia another hug and wished her a good night.

Herding Ethan and Heather inside, Olivia sent Heather to

her room for bed, despite her protests. "I'm not tired! Can't I stay up and watch a movie?"

"It's already past your bedtime, and it's been an extremely full day. Tomorrow, we don't have anything going on, so we can talk about watching a movie after breakfast."

"Fine," Heather grumbled. "Goodnight."

Olivia and Ethan exchanged an amused glance as Heather's shoulders wilted, and she shuffled to her room. Olivia said in a low voice, "She'll be as good as new after a good night's sleep. She'll probably fall asleep before she blinks twice."

"I think she was on to something, though," Ethan said, jabbing his thumb toward the living room. "Wanna unwind and watch a movie?"

Olivia smiled at him. "You read my mind."

Popping a pan of popcorn and grabbing two cans of soda from the fridge, they settled next to each other on the couch. Ethan grabbed the remote, and for five minutes, they laughed and teased each other over movie suggestions.

"Alright, alright," Ethan said, conceding. "We'll watch your sappy Christmas romance because it is Christmas in a week."

"Thank you," Olivia said, tugging the remote out of his hand and selecting the movie.

The opening credits started, and they watched together without speaking, eating popcorn and putting up their aching feet. The Christmas tree Olivia had put up in the corner cast a warm glow in the dimly lit room, and she'd hung an extra stocking for Ethan on the mantle. She knew it was silly and premature of her to wonder what life would be like as a whole family again, but she couldn't keep her mind from wandering down that path after seeing the magnitude of generosity Ethan had arranged on her behalf. Even though Jeff had turned his back on his family, Olivia was sure there were still happily ever afters still out there. Ethan was proving it to her on a daily basis.

Ethan put his arm up over the back of the couch and gently drew Olivia over to him. Adjusting the blanket over them both, Olivia tipped her head under his arm, where she listened to the steady rhythm of his heart.

"How on earth did you pull it off?" Olivia asked. "I have a hard time believing you didn't dip into your charity's funds to pay for at least a box of nails for my roof."

"You want me to have Emma send the financial records?" Ethan asked. "She'll talk your ear off for hours about numbers if you really want her to."

"That's alright." Olivia laughed. "I think I'm in shock. It's just the biggest gift anyone has ever given me."

"Twila was right. You deserved it." Ethan kissed her on the top of her head and drew in a breath of her hair. "You want to know why it was possible to get you a new roof?"

Olivia nibbled on her lower lip and looked up at Ethan. "Sure. Put my curiosity to rest."

"Because, people in this town love you. It didn't take hardly any effort to get volunteers to come do the work. Twila and Heather made a few phone calls, and it kind of took off. People were calling us to offer their help."

"That was sweet of them," Olivia murmured.

"It was the same with supplies. Several of the home improvement stores donated materials, people brought their ladders, and for what was left, people freely gave their money."

Olivia played with a loose thread on the blanket. "I guess I never really thought I was that memorable."

"Olivia," Ethan said, lacing his fingers through hers, "it is nice to be able to do those grandiose things that feel like they're big and meaningful, but most of the time, it's the small things that stick with people."

"Maybe."

"Think of me, for example."

"What about you? You know I feed all my paying guests as well as I've been feeding you."

His smirk grew, making Olivia's heart flutter. "That's kind of what I mean. You might not think it means a lot, but I can tell the way you make food, that you pour yourself into it. That's how you show people you love them. I mean, even the first time we met at the diner, I was being a total jerk, but you saw through it and that I had a need, and served me the best hot chocolate I've ever had. Money can't buy that kind of service."

A deep breath swept through Olivia. "Part of my frustration at being not as financially well-off as I'd like is that I don't have the funds to help *more* people. I could fix up this place so it's more comfortable for my guests, so that when they're here, the outside world is kept at bay. Then maybe I'd also be able to help others who are in the same sort of situation I am. I think that's definitely one appeal of being wealthy. That I'd have so much more to be able to give."

Ethan quirked an eyebrow at her. "You wouldn't mind being rich?"

Olivia laughed at his question. "Mind? No, I guess not. But I still fear that attachment that so many people have to money. When they don't have it, they think having it will fix everything in their life. When they do have it, they think they're somehow better than everyone, because God gave them that particular challenge."

"What do you mean it's a challenge?"

"Well," Olivia said. "I imagine having a lot of money is a big responsibility. That would scare me about having a huge bank account. I suppose I don't have to worry about that though. I doubt I'm ever going to be rich in a traditional sense off a bed and breakfast. Not unless I turn it into an establishment where the rich and famous come to vacation."

Ethan chuckled and stroked Olivia's hair. "You never know. You playing the violin at the Christmas tree lighting seemed to draw a big crowd. Rich people like those kind of quaint, small-town traditions."

"And how would you know?" Olivia asked, poking her finger into his abs.

He rubbed his finger across his lips and glanced over at the movie. "Emma and I run with some pretty wealthy people, and that's what she says about them, especially after she was able to stay here for a few days herself. She's already been recommending you to everyone she's met."

"Huh. Well, whatever life throws at me, I think I'm learning to be content with a comfortable existence."

Ethan nodded and seemed to retreat into his own thoughts. "I have a confession to make."

His words made Olivia's spine stiffen. "What is it? Please don't tell me you have some skeletons in your closet. You aren't already married or something, are you?"

Ethan laughed so loud it made Olivia's face burn with humiliation for even asking. "No. Nothing quite like that. I was just going to say that it's true I didn't use my charity's funds for anything, I technically did use some of my own personal money for help on the roof."

"You lied to me?"

Holding up his hands, he quickly added, "It's not what you think. I bought lunch for everyone who came. Oh, and a small gift of appreciation for Twila. Nothing too exorbitant. It was something she mentioned. It should arrive just in time for Christmas."

"She'll love it, I'm sure." Olivia sighed contently and nestled in closer to Ethan. "You know what I appreciate, even more than the new roof?"

"What?"

"The feeling of being loved. So many people gave their time and energy for me. It was the kind of assurance I needed that I'm not overlooked."

"I get that," Ethan said softly. "I'm happy to be able to have had a small hand in it." Ethan hesitated. "Speaking of love…"

The word made Olivia's pulse take off, and she could barely hear anything else around the thundering of her heart. "Yes?"

"I know it's been such a short time, and I don't want it to be uncomfortable but…I love you, Olivia." He put his hand on her cheek. "I'm surer of it every day."

Olivia's voice felt so small as she answered. "I love you, too, Ethan. I've wanted to tell you, too, but couldn't find the courage to say it out loud. I thought I was silly for even thinking it, but there was something I couldn't put my finger on that drew me to you, even from the beginning. Aside from your good looks, of course. But that's an obvious attraction any hot-blooded woman would have."

"I'll be sure to watch out for other women," Ethan teased.

Poking him in the ribs, Olivia continued, "The more we've gotten to spend time together, and the more I've gotten to know you, I've come to realize you're a very real answer to my prayers."

Ethan leaned in and kissed her with such passion Olivia was afraid she wouldn't be able to catch her breath. He pulled back but kept her enveloped in his arms. "That's all I've ever wanted. To be loved as I am."

CHAPTER 15

"I heard through the grapevine that Mallory's been asking about you," Emma said.

Ethan switched the phone from one shoulder to the other as he pulled on a button-up shirt after his shower. He'd slept a little later than he'd intended, but the long day before had taken its toll. Glancing at the clock, he could see it was already nine. Chances were, even if Olivia liked to sleep in, it was late enough that she was already awake in the kitchen. He mentally kicked himself for wasting any time he could have had with her today before he had to leave for Seattle.

He groaned and dropped down onto his bed. "Don't ruin my good mood."

"She's been throwing a tantrum around town, trying to figure out where you are."

"You didn't say anything, did you?"

Emma scoffed defensively. "Rude. Obviously not. You really think I'd encourage her hunt for you when I like the girl you've chosen now so much more? Olivia is way out of your league, so consider it a blessing she picked you."

Ethan smiled at the words. He was glad it was so obvious

to everyone. Mallory may have made sense from a logical standpoint, but Olivia made his heart complete. That's what he needed.

"I think so, too."

"You haven't botched it up since I left, have you? She still likes you for who you are, right?"

"Now it's my turn to be offended," Ethan said with a laugh. "You really think I'm that much of an idiot that I'd throw something as good as Olivia away?"

"You are a dude…"

"Thanks for the vote of confidence."

Emma giggled. "Seriously. You know what I mean. You're not just any old guy, and that has the potential to scare away some women."

"Really? Because being a billionaire CEO of a huge company seems to attract more women than it deflects."

"The wrong kind of women. Take Mallory for example."

Ethan put on a touch of cologne before running a comb through his damp hair. "Well, Olivia loves me the way I am without knowing my net worth, so I'm assuming her finding out I have a bit more in my bank account than she probably suspects isn't going to be *that* big of a problem."

"Wait a sec. Did she tell you she loves you?"

"Yes. Last night, in fact. I said I loved her first, and she reciprocated."

Ethan's heart soared as he recalled it. He'd never been so worried about another person's answer as he had been wondering what Olivia would say. Not even when he proposed marriage to Mallory. With Olivia, he felt absolutely vulnerable and scared out of his wits, but the moment she looked into his eyes, he knew his heart was safe with her. After they'd confessed their feelings for each other and shared a few more kisses, they'd cuddled for the rest of the movie. By the time the credits were rolling, Olivia had dozed off. In his last act of service to her that day, he'd carefully carried her to bed, covered her with a blanket, and wished her sweet dreams with a kiss on her forehead.

Emma gasped. "Way to go, Ethan! I didn't know you had it in you!"

"It's true," Ethan said with a chuckle. "I have a heart."

"Well, you can thank me for unfolding the mysteries of the female mind to you. I hope now you fully appreciate having a sister to guide you."

Ethan rolled his eyes. Glancing at himself in the mirror, satisfied he was presentable, he headed for the door.

"I'll be sure to buy you something over-the-top and outrageous to show my appreciation for you this Christmas. But right now, I've got to go. I don't want to waste my last day with Olivia for a while talking on the phone with you."

"Fine. I'll see you tomorrow. Peg said the jet is scheduled to pick you up from the airport around six."

Ethan said goodbye to his sister and flew down the stairs and headed to the kitchen, where heavenly smells of peppers and bacon were wafting through the air. He wasn't looking forward to having to leave, but he was going to make good use of his remaining time in Holly Wreath, especially fitting in as many heart stopping kisses with Olivia as he could manage.

"Good morning," Olivia said as she stood by the stove, stirring a frying pan of scrambled eggs. "Hope you don't mind, but I'm going lowkey this morning. Scrambled eggs with some veggies, cheese, and bacon. The toast should be ready soon, too."

Strolling over to her, he snuggled up behind her and kissed her on her temple, then down her cheek and to her neck, eliciting a shriek from her.

She swatted him away with her spatula. "Your scruff tickles!"

Ethan ran his hand down his cheeks. "You prefer me clean shaven?"

Olivia shrugged. "I do love a good five o'clock shadow, but if you're going to be nuzzling up to my neck, and you don't want me screaming and squirming because I'm ticklish, then you'll have to shave."

"Duly noted," Ethan said. Noticing Heather was missing, he asked where she was.

"She left twenty minutes ago to watch a movie at a friend's house," Olivia said, turning off the stove and putting the eggs on the table. "I think she's still angry at me for not letting her stay up last night."

"If she was anything like me, she slept like a rock."

"It was a long, glorious day yesterday but extremely tiring. I know she was exhausted, too," Olivia said. Suddenly appearing shy, she looked sideways at Ethan. "Thanks, by the way."

"For what?"

"For carrying me to bed after I drifted off to sleep. I was kind of surprised I didn't wake up on the couch this morning. I would've been fine if you would have tossed a blanket over me and left me there."

Ethan waved his hand, dismissing her comment. "You wouldn't have slept as well and would've probably woken up with a crick in your neck. I was happy to take you to your room."

Helping put stuff out on the table, Ethan and Olivia sat down to eat together when Olivia's phone rang in her apron pocket. She frowned slightly but stood up as she looked at the screen. "Will you excuse me? I'm expecting a call from someone who made an online registration, and I think this is them."

"Take your time," Ethan said. "I'm not going anywhere."

Olivia grinned and gave him a quick kiss on the cheek

before she trotted out of the room and down the hall to a small office she kept for running the business side of the Holly Wreath Inn.

It wasn't two minutes later that the back door swung open and shut. "Heather?" Ethan asked, leaning back in his chair to see if he could see who'd come in.

Twila sauntered through the mudroom door with the strangest smirk on her face. Unwinding the scarf she'd looped around her neck, she had a magazine tucked under her arm and her purse on the other.

"Good morning, Ethan Wilder," Twila said, letting his name roll very deliberately off her tongue.

Ice seeped into every inch of Ethan's veins as he knew she knew. Trying to play ignorant to her amusement, Ethan asked, "Is it chilly out there today? I haven't been outside yet."

"Yep. A real cold snap is blowing through again, reminding everyone that at least in Holly Wreath, it's December."

"Well, I guess no one can complain, can they? It's no worse than it was last week. Think you'll get snow here for Christmas?"

"Perhaps," Twila said. She reached for the magazine under her arm. "I know I sure had to bundle up to run to the grocery store this morning."

"Oh, yeah? Any good sales?"

"A few. What was really interesting about my trip was when I was checking out. I spotted this on the shelf."

She tossed the magazine on the table, and it slid to a stop right in front of Ethan. A picture of him in his suit, talking on a cell phone as he was leaving the office was front and center. The yellow title in block letters—*Billionaire Ethan Wilder has a Broken Heart...and is Single Again*—made Ethan want to shrink under a rock. His life had followed him to Holly Wreath whether he wanted it to or not.

"Look. I can explain."

Twila held her hand up. "There's nothing to explain, Ethan. I told you I knew I'd seen your face before, I just couldn't remember where. You're the billionaire every single woman in America has her eye on."

Ethan's blood pressure skyrocketed, and he wasn't sure how he was going to placate Twila enough to ensure she wouldn't tell Olivia about that part of himself. "I'm sorry I didn't tell you sooner. I was enjoying a bit of anonymity. It's not often that I get to leave the public persona the media has created behind."

Twila's blue gray eyes were penetrating. "You don't have to apologize to me. You're still the same Ethan I met two weeks ago. Question is, does Olivia know?"

He blew a breath out through his lips and shook his head. "Not yet."

Twila's eyebrows shot up almost to her hairline. "If there's one thing you need to know about Olivia, it's that she doesn't like secrets."

"I know." Ethan slumped in his seat. "I didn't mean to keep anything from her, but things have been a whirlwind. Honestly, I was planning on testing the waters and mentioning it to her today before I had to leave. I was just trying to figure out how to bring it up."

Twila sat down at the seat on the opposite side and put her hand on his. "Listen. I'm not trying to rat you out to her. What you two have together is something special, and I've rarely seen Olivia so happy. I don't want you to mess it up because you're keeping a part of yourself from her."

Ethan laughed humorlessly. "You're starting to sound like my sister."

"I'll take that as a compliment," Twila said, patting his hand and sliding the magazine back to her side. "So is this headline true? You're nursing a broken heart here?"

"I left Seattle to clear my head. I wouldn't exactly say it was because I had a broken heart. More grumpy about life in general. But Olivia's turned me around."

"You are a lot less uptight around her, that's for certain."

Ethan could hear Olivia down the hallway shut the door to her office, and the blood drained out of his face. Twila grabbed her magazine and tucked it back under her arm, winking at Ethan.

"Good news!" Olivia said, clasping her hands together as she walked back into the kitchen. "That was another person. I have another guest that'll be arriving tomorrow. He's kicking off the start of being booked solid for two months, beginning right after Christmas."

"That's really great," Ethan said. "I'm happy for you."

Twila stood up and gave Olivia a quick squeeze. "Things are looking up for you. I'm so glad."

"Thanks, Twila."

"I'd love to stay and socialize, but I have a trunkful of groceries that aren't going to unload themselves," Twila said. Reaching for the scarf she'd laid across the back of her chair, she dropped the magazine.

"What's this?" Olivia said, kneeling down to pick it up. "I never pegged you for one of those ladies that read celebrity magazines, Twila. It's all gossip anyway."

Ethan thought about snatching the magazine out of her hands but stopped himself. That would only make him look desperate and guilty when she figured out what he was trying to conceal. Watching her turn over the magazine was like watching a car wreck happen. Reading the cover, she froze, the smile slipping off her face.

"Ethan…?" Her blue eyes rushed to his, and she held the magazine up for him to see. The photo the magazine had chosen made him look like a rich, arrogant, condescending snob. "Is this you?"

Words failed him. He wasn't ashamed of his wealth, but he'd mislead Olivia. Money certainly didn't define him, but he knew it did for the way other people saw him.

"I was going to tell you," he said, licking his lips and staring unblinkingly at her. "I knew it would be a bit of a shock when you found out, so I wanted to be the one who told you. When the time was right."

Olivia turned the magazine back around, not saying a word. She reread the cover, and that made him cringe. More than his money, the media painting him as broken-hearted and unhappy that he was fresh out of a committed relationship was a concern. He didn't want Olivia in any way to feel like he was using her to remedy his disappointment.

"You're the billionaire everyone's been talking about?" Olivia asked. He nodded. "It's been all over the radio and television, but I never paid any attention to it because the last place I figured he'd end up would be in Holly Wreath."

"I didn't think I'd be here long myself, but I've loved every second of it in Holly Wreath."

He stepped forward to take her hand, but she shied away, taking a step back herself. His heart raced in his chest, and it felt like his ribs might be fractured as it slammed against them. Olivia was slipping away from him, and the thought of losing her made panic swell from within.

"Am I the rebound?" Olivia asked. "It says here you're heartbroken and single. Or at least you were when you left Seattle."

Ethan held up his hands. "No, you're nothing like that. Yes, I left Seattle to clear my head after my fiancée left me, but I'm anything but heartbroken."

Olivia's eyes widened and she stumbled over her words. "Your fiancée? You were engaged?"

The room felt ten degrees too warm, and sweat seeped

out of every one of his pores. "Briefly. It was a precarious relationship at best."

"I'd hardly call agreeing to marry precarious," Olivia said.

"You're right," Ethan said, wanting to be as agreeable as possible to smooth the whole situation over. "What I mean is that our relationship was based on business more than anything. Her father owned a programming company that was going to be beneficial for my company." Ethan couldn't believe how ridiculous it sounded, saying the words out loud. "We got along well enough, but the longer it's been since she left me, the more positive I am ours wasn't a love match. I'm not attached to her at all. It's in the past."

Olivia's shock gave way to anger, and she trembled as it built up. "This is exactly what I said I hated about money. People like you who have it, think they're above everyone else because their bank accounts are bursting at the seams, and that they can lie and conceal and deceive."

She jabbed her finger into his chest with every word, but he took it, hoping if she spilled all of her emotions that she'd calm down enough to realize that he'd made a mistake but that he was the same man who still loved her.

"I'm sorry, Olivia. I didn't mean to hurt you."

"But you did," Olivia snapped, blinking back tears. "I shared my secrets with you, but you purposefully kept some very large secrets away from me to conceal who you really are. You were engaged to be married! You couldn't have at least mentioned that?"

Ethan ran a hand through his hair. "I didn't think it would have made any difference. My fiancée and I are through. She's in the past."

Olivia opened her mouth to continue but was stopped short by the doorbell.

Twila, who'd been watching everything unfold with horror, stepped forward and offered, "I'll get it."

"No," Olivia said, her voice cracking. "It's my house, I'll get it. It'll give me a second to calm down after realizing a person I cared about so much lied to me."

She'd meant for her words to cut deep, and they did. Olivia hurried to the front door, smoothing her hands over her hair and tugging down her shirt. Ethan was drawn after her. Yes, she was ticked at him, but if he let her get too far from him, it seemed as if their connection would break. The doorbell rang again, and she picked up the pace, reaching for the doorknob.

She swung it open and Ethan's heart froze.

Mallory had found him.

"Hello, can I help you?"

Mallory was in impossibly high stiletto boots and a mini skirt intended to show off her legs, with only a white, feathery coat over a slinky blouse to keep warm. She pushed her way into the foyer, shivering and cursing under her breath about the wind.

"About time you answered the door. I about died of hypoperm...hydrotherm...I about died of cold waiting out there."

"I'm sorry. I wasn't expecting anyone this morning," Olivia said. Ethan had to hand it to her for being so cordial after she'd been raking him across the coals.

"I didn't make a reservation or anything." Looking around the room in thinly-veiled disgust, Mallory spotted Ethan standing in the shadows. Pointing a long, glittery mauve nail at him, she said, "I'm here for him."

Olivia glanced back at Ethan with a look of bewilderment. "You know Ethan?"

"I'd better," she said, her full lips splitting into a smile. "I'm Mallory, his fiancée."

173

CHAPTER 16

Olivia grabbed onto a stair railing to steady herself, afraid she might pass out. She'd woken up refreshed and excited about the day, and in a matter of an hour, it was in shambles. Even though Ethan was going back to Seattle, and she would miss having him with her, his confession of love had made her excited for the future possibilities. Standing in the foyer with his former fiancée, who was obviously not as over their relationship as Ethan claimed, Olivia felt like the other woman.

Mallory shrugged off her fluffy coat, revealing the rest of a skin-tight top covered in shimmering silver sequins. "Do you know how long it took for me to find you? I looked in all your usual Washington hideouts and practically lived at your apartment waiting for you to show up, but when you didn't come home, I knew I was going to have to come find you."

The room started to spin, and Olivia's stomach roiled sickeningly. Twila stepped in, covering for Olivia while she tried to regain her composure. "Can I make you a cup of herbal tea to warm up? Or a blueberry scone? I believe Olivia has some left over from yesterday's breakfast."

Mallory tipped her head back and laughed. "That won't be necessary. I don't need all those calories going to my hips. It takes an incredible amount of self-control to keep this figure."

She gestured her hands up and down her body, rubbing in how glamorous and composed she was. Olivia could see why Ethan had chosen her. Mallory was the kind of girl he could take to galas and would take good photographs for magazine spreads. Looking down at her own calloused hands, Olivia knew she was too rough around the edges and plain for the glitz of Ethan's world.

"So, no tea?" Twila reiterated.

"Thanks, but no," Mallory said without a hint of sincerity. "I'd like a private moment with Ethan, if you don't mind."

"Let us know if there's anything we can help with," Twila said, walking over to Olivia and tugging on her elbow.

Olivia was rooted in place. She was watching her worst nightmare unfold but couldn't bring herself to look away.

Ethan hadn't said a word since Olivia had opened the door, but he found his voice when Mallory stepped closer and tried to take his hand. "What are you doing here?"

"I'm here to rescue you, silly. It took me long enough to find you, you know that?" Mallory poked him playfully on the shoulder. "I asked your secretary where you'd gone, but she wouldn't tell me. You really should have Peg fired. You don't have time for that kind of belligerence."

"I asked her not to tell anyone," Ethan said. He clenched his jaw together and worked the muscles as he glared at Mallory. "In case you're forgetting, you ran off with a guy I knew in college and sent a very clear text that we were through."

Mallory giggled and twirled a lock of her amber hair behind her right ear. "It was cold feet. You know people do all sorts of ridiculous things when they're scared. I can be the bigger person and take full responsibility, but I'm ready to move on now that it's all out of my system."

As furious as Olivia was at Ethan, she felt a twinge of pity for him. "You ran off with one of his friends?"

Mallory's brown eyes flashed to Olivia, and Mallory narrowed them to slits. "A little privacy, please?" Turning back to Ethan, she scoffed and muttered, "Real charming place you chose."

Any patience Olivia might've had had already evaporated listening to Ethan in the kitchen, but before she could tear Mallory to shreds with her words, Twila excused them both and yanked them to the kitchen.

"What are you doing?" Olivia hissed. "I had a right to stay there."

"Sometimes, biting your tongue hurts," Twila whispered. Her eyes were full of a compassion that should have disarmed Olivia—and would have—if her anger wasn't already boiling within. "It wouldn't do you any good ripping that girl apart. You'd feel bad afterwards; she'd feel bad. She and Ethan need to work it out."

Olivia scoffed and went to the fridge where she pulled out a batch of peanut butter fudge she'd made with Ethan and Heather, then grabbed a large spoon from the drawer. She slammed it shut, making the silverware clatter out of the tray. From the entryway, she could still hear Ethan and Mallory's hushed, tense voices. She couldn't discern what they were saying, but it was clear they were arguing. Scooping up a spoonful directly from the pan, she took an enormous bite.

"That's the problem. Ethan hasn't exactly proven himself to be trustworthy. Who knows if they'll work it out? I'm not okay with being the girl on the side for him."

"No one would expect you to be, and that doesn't seem like what Ethan wants either," Twila said.

Olivia ate another mouthful of fudge. "His fiancée begs to differ, and so does your magazine."

Twila hesitated but put her hand on Olivia's shoulder and gave her a gentle shake. "I think I know what this is really about."

"And what's that?"

"Not every man is like Jeff."

"And not every relationship is like your marriage. I'm happy for you, that you had decades of wedded bliss, but not all of us are so lucky." The words were acrid, and she regretted them the second she said them, but the bitterness brewing in her soul pushed them out.

"I know I was blessed, and because I know how good a healthy, happy relationship can be, I hope that for everyone." Twila swallowed back tears and gave Olivia a shaky smile. "I don't want to preach at you, though. If you need any help or a shoulder to cry on, you know where to find me."

Twila let herself out the back, and Olivia sank into a chair at the kitchen table, her chin quivering as she took a ragged breath. Twila hadn't deserved to be on the receiving end of her resentment, but Olivia's world was spiraling so fast, and feeling wounded, she'd lashed out without thinking.

Eating another bite of fudge, it renewed the feeling that she was going to be sick to her stomach. The voices of Mallory and Ethan were gone from the foyer. They'd gone upstairs to Ethan's room where, no matter how solid the doors were, their heated shouting could be heard.

Putting the lid back on the fudge, Olivia sank down, pressing her forehead to the table and wrapping her arms around her head, blocking out the light as she tried to process the morning. Strong emotions collided until she couldn't stand it anymore. Shooting up out of her chair, she went to get her coat, purse, and keys.

"Where are you going?" Ethan asked from the doorway.

He watched her with pleading, worried, hollow eyes. She turned away from him, afraid her resolve might falter if she was looking at him.

"I'm going to run some errands, so I'll leave you and your fiancée to it. Like Mallory said, you could use some privacy." She put on her coat and zipped it up. "I hope you have a safe trip home. I'm sure you know your way out."

Striding to the door, Ethan caught up and tugged her back to him. Before he could disarm her with a hug, she pushed his hands away and retreated.

"Don't leave," he begged. "We need to talk."

"I think you've probably got your hands full needing to talk to Mallory. It sounds like there's plenty of unfinished business with her."

Ethan raked a hand through his hair. "I already sent her home. I think she's finally understanding that there's no coming back from her betrayal."

Olivia huffed. "That's funny. I've sort of been thinking the same thing about you."

Ethan closed off, crossing his arms as he spoke. "How is what I did even remotely close to what Mallory did to me?"

Olivia's face grew warm. "Seriously? You're not connecting it? That you're both liars?"

"No," Ethan shot back, "I omitted the fact that I *was* once engaged, and that I'm a billionaire. Mallory ran off with another guy because she decided I wasn't good enough for her. Two totally different situations."

"Whatever makes you feel better."

"What do you want?" Ethan asked, his voice raising and holding his hands expectantly. "Since when has being well-off been a bad thing? Because I guarantee you wouldn't want people judging you unfairly because you're not as rich as I am."

"I work just as hard as you," Olivia said tersely.

"Nobody's questioning that. So why are you holding it against me that I've worked hard, too, and have been able to make my family's business into something?"

"Why couldn't you say it? Why was it something you had to keep from me, then?"

Ethan shrugged, struggling to get the words out. "I liked being known for who I am, not for what I have. You couldn't possibly understand how hard it is to get close to people when they're always using you for your money."

"So, you think I'm like everyone else? Petty and shallow?" Olivia asked, putting her hands on her hips.

"How was I supposed to know when I first met you? You think I walk up to people, tell them I'm Ethan Wilder, billionaire CEO of Seattle's biggest tech company as an introduction?"

Olivia scoffed, tossing her hair behind her shoulder. "Maybe not, but I kind of got the impression after you kissed me and told me that you loved me that I wasn't some nobody you just met off the street."

"That's true," Ethan said. "I should have told you. I was waiting for the right time, that's all."

"You probably should've mentioned your past before your fiancée showed up on my doorstep looking for you," Olivia said. She knew she was punching below the belt, but it didn't matter. She wanted it to hurt.

"This is exactly what I was afraid of happening. If I would've told you when we first met, then you would've kept your walls up, and I never would have gotten to know you. So I kept it to myself, and you accuse me of being a liar and selfish. Do you see the bind I'm in?"

Olivia dropped her head as tears stung her eyes. She was so mad and confused that she could barely make a coherent thought. "And what about my roof? I suppose you enjoy giving big, over-the-top gifts so you can feel better about yourself?"

"Olivia," Ethan said tersely, "do you even hear what you're saying? It's ridiculous. Unlike you, I don't need other people's approval to be happy."

She knew she was clinging to her pride, unwilling to admit she had any part in the chasm growing in their relationship, but she felt like the kitchen was stifling. Ethan's words had struck a nerve, and it hurt because she knew he was right. "I need to get out of here."

Ethan's eyes widened, and he took a tentative step forward. "Please. Not yet. I don't have to go to the airport for another four hours. We can talk this over. Work it out."

"I'm not sure there is a solution," Olivia said. "We're from two different worlds. Consider it a holiday fling. Thanks for everything you've done, but I can handle it from here."

"But this can't be it. I love you, Olivia."

Shaking her head, Olivia said, "We barely know each other."

"We can still try," Ethan said.

The pleading in his face made Olivia's heart crack and her resolve falter until her hardened heart made her turn away. "I don't think that's possible. I think you were in love with the idea of me, but when it comes down to the raw, honest truth, we're too different."

Without another word, she spun on her heels and hurried out the back, slamming the door hard like it was responsible for her being unlucky in love. Fumbling with her keys, she unlocked her car, praying for it to start—she knew the battery needed to be replaced, and it could be sluggish when it was cold—and it mercifully roared to life.

She caught a glimpse of Ethan in the window, and he appeared like the shell of his former self. The image haunted her as she put her car in drive and sped away to nowhere in particular.

Tears and a soft flurry of snowflakes made it difficult to see. She parked the car at a nearby park and rested her forehead on the steering wheel as sobs shook her whole body. What Jeff had done had left her emotionally scarred, and she knew she was guarded, but she couldn't bring herself to let that kind of betrayal go. Was she wrong for wanting to have someone she could trust? Or were relationships like that all an illusion?

After idling in the car for an hour and feeling completely drained, she decided to go back to the inn to see if Ethan had left. All she wanted to do was lie on her bed and sleep away the throbbing headache that made it feel like she had a vice around her temples. If she was being honest, she almost hoped that he was still there so she could let him take her in his arms, walk her to the couch, and sooth her concerns. They had both had a moment of weakness where they said things that were unfair.

She held back, though, unsure she could survive another failed relationship.

Pulling to a stop along the curb a block away from the Holly Wreath Inn, Olivia could see the BMW was still parked in the driveway. While she sat and observed, she admired the new roof on the house, and imagined how magnificent it would look the following spring when she used her tax return to give it a fresh coat of paint. The decorative trim would be painted in an accent color, and she was debating painting the rest of it a pretty blue.

She sighed. Even if she worked double shifts at the diner, she wasn't sure she could ever repay the debt she owed to Ethan, and even if she could, she'd never be able to look at the house without thinking of him.

Her hammering heartbeat made her headache worse, and

she tried to work up the courage to go and apologize for her stubbornness when Ethan walked out the door, pulling his small suitcase behind him. Olivia was frozen in place, too scared to get out of her car or call for him. He turned to look at the house, standing in the driveway for a long time, like he was trying to soak in every last detail of the bed and breakfast.

Then just like that, he got in his car and drove away, taking a piece of Olivia's heart along with him. Touching her head back to the steering wheel, Olivia let the tears fall anew.

CHAPTER 17

"Wake up, sleepyhead."

Ethan refused to open his eyes even though Emma had pulled open his curtains, and a rare sunny winter day in Seattle nearly blinded him through his pinched eyelids. She wiggled his shoulder, and he responded by rolling over and pulling the sheets over his head.

"Don't say I didn't warn you," Emma said.

Ethan peeked out from under the sheets to see what she was doing and was met with a pillow to the face. She got in three solid whacks before he wrestled the pillow away and tossed it across the room.

"I'm up, alright?" Ethan croaked. He reached for a glass of water on his nightstand and downed it in two gulps.

"Good. Getting you out of bed was the first thing on my to-do list today," Emma said looking entirely too pleased with herself.

"You and your to-do lists," Ethan said as he swung his feet out of bed.

Emma brushed a fuzz off her skirt. "It keeps me organized and motivated."

"Good for you," Ethan said. He picked up a sweatshirt from off the floor and sniffed it to make sure it was clean enough. Satisfied, he pulled it over his head. "Is there something you wanted? Because I finished up everything I needed to do in-office last night around midnight. I'm working from home today."

Emma folded her arms and looked at him, expectantly raising her eyebrows.

"What?" Ethan asked.

She picked up another throw pillow from off the armchair in his bedroom and chucked it at him. "You know what. You still haven't told me what happened with Olivia. You can't hide behind the guise of work, and I can tell you're back to your typical broody self."

The shadow of a cloud passed over the sun, and Ethan couldn't help but chuckle bitterly at the irony of how her name could both make him want to run all the way back to Holly Wreath to scoop her up in his arms, while at the same time want to climb under the covers and never leave his apartment again.

"There's not a whole lot to say. She found out who I am and wanted nothing more to do with me."

Emma tsked and rolled her eyes. "I highly doubt that's *all* that happened."

Ethan wandered to his kitchen and picked up a stack of mail he'd grabbed from his mailbox but hadn't sorted through yet. "It probably didn't help that Mallory showed up."

"Mallory?" Emma asked, her mouth falling open. "How'd she find you?"

"You're sure you didn't even give her a hint where I was?"

Emma held her hand to her chest, and Ethan knew he'd offended her. "Me? No. Why on earth would I try to sabotage the best thing that's ever happened to you?"

"I don't know," Ethan grunted, ripping up the junk mail and tossing it in his recycling bin.

"Wait a minute," Emma said, intuitively dissecting the situation. "I'm guessing Mallory showing up was such a big deal because you never told Olivia you were engaged. Am I right?"

Ethan took in a breath. "It never came up."

Emma threw her hands in the air. "Ethan! You've got to be one of the biggest idiots I know. You didn't think it was pertinent information that your engagement had recently been broken off? And then Olivia had to find out about it coming face to face with Mallory? You're lucky Olivia didn't dump gasoline on your belongings and set them on fire."

Ethan tensed, and hot anger ripped through him. "Look, I know I royally screwed up. I don't need you to tell me that. The one chance I had with someone I truly cared about slipped through my fingers because I didn't fully trust her. So, thanks for the reminder that yet again, Christmas is going to be miserable."

Ethan's outburst quieted Emma, and he pretended not to notice her eyes were on him while he prepared himself a protein shake for breakfast. He didn't mind that that was all he had in his pantry, but he would have much preferred Olivia's home cooking. A veggie omelet oozing with melted cheese and a slice of homemade bread would've hit the spot.

"Ethan, I know you have a tedious relationship with Christmas, especially because of our parents' deaths—"

"Don't forget Mallory humiliating me this year," Ethan said as he took a long draw of his drink. "That wasn't exactly an awesome kickoff to the season."

"If you want to get technical, that was around Thanksgiving, not Christmas, since she ran off with Derek right after my wedding," Emma said.

Ethan shrugged. "Potato, potahto."

Emma took a seat at the marble slab island and lined up his salt and pepper shakers with the napkin holder. "The point I'm trying to make is that it doesn't have to be this way. You were so close to having the best Christmas of your life, but from the sounds of it, you kind of gave up."

"I didn't give up. She made it pretty clear she was done with me."

"No," Emma corrected. "It sounds like she was mad. Nobody makes good decisions when they're upset. And she's not totally wrong, either."

"So what do you think I'm supposed to do? Crawl back to her on my hands and knees and hope she doesn't slam the door in my face? She's already done that once before, so I know she's capable of doing it again."

"Groveling might not be a bad start. At least then she'll know you're serious," Emma said with a teasing smile. Ethan chuckled at his ridiculous sister and finished off his breakfast drink. "But seriously, I've never known you to be one who quit so easily when you set your sights on something."

"Maybe," Ethan said. "The problem is, I'm not sure how I'll cope if she doesn't want me. I can't imagine a life without her, and that terrifies me."

Emma's sly smile grew, and she nodded. "That seems like a pretty telltale sign of how you really feel."

Ethan gazed out at the panoramic views of his apartment overlooking Seattle. It was impressive for sure, but he would have traded it all to be curled up with Olivia on the couch by her Christmas tree, propping her feet up on his lap, and laughing together while Heather regaled them with her hilarious retellings of what had happened that day in school.

"What am I supposed to do to win her back and show her I'm in it for the long haul?"

Emma leaned onto the counter and folded her arms. "I can't answer that for you."

"Thanks for the help," Ethan said with a scoff.

"I'm not trying to make it hard for you."

"Well, you are. You're supposed to help me untangle the feminine mystique so I have a fighting chance. That's what you're always telling me you're good for."

Emma raised her shoulders and let them fall. "I'll let you in on a secret—women aren't as complicated as men think we are."

"Says a woman," Ethan said miserably.

"My point is, you know Olivia better than I do. If I try to dictate what to do to try and make it right, it'd come off as ingenuine and counterfeit. It wouldn't be you."

"So you're saying you're not going to help me?"

"Obviously," Emma said, nudging her shoulder into his. "All I came over to do was to make sure you were at least *trying* to win her back."

Ethan narrowed his eyes at her. "Why are you so interested in my love life?"

"Because. I like Olivia. I could see myself being best friends with her, and Heather is absolutely adorable. Reminds me of what I was like twenty years ago."

"So, your interest in my relationship with her is purely selfish?"

"Not really," Emma said. "I'll be friends with her no matter what you do. In fact, Rob and I already have a reservation at her inn this spring."

Ethan chuckled and shook his head. "Have fun with that."

"I want you to work it out with Olivia because I've never seen you so happy as you were with her. It's like you're a totally different person. You're lighthearted and friendly, and aren't afraid to laugh. That's the gift I want for you this Christmas. To love and be loved. You deserve that happiness, and so does Olivia."

Ethan bounced his leg. Hope had seeded itself in his

heart, and he dared to let himself believe it was possible. "Christmas Eve is tomorrow."

"And?" Emma said with a laugh. "You have all the resources of a billionaire at your fingertips."

Ethan stood up and paced the length of his penthouse apartment, bumping his thumb against his lips. "Is the jet available tomorrow?"

Emma leapt out of her seat and flung her arms around Ethan's neck. "You're going to go for it?"

"I'll regret it if I don't."

"Good," Emma said, giving him a squeeze around his arms. "I'm going to go tell Rob."

"You do that."

"Oh, don't be jealous," Emma said, pinching his cheek. "If you don't totally mess this up, you'll have the same thing with Olivia that Rob and I enjoy."

"If I'm lucky," Ethan answered.

Emma grabbed her purse and trench coat off the table by his entry. Practically floating out the door, she poked her head back in. "Keep me apprised. I want in on this Christmas miracle."

Ethan assured her he would, and when he finally shooed her out the door, he hustled to set his plan in motion. He made a phone call to Peg, apologizing for asking her to run some errands for him, but she reminded him just how much he was paying her, and since that was funding her daughter's college education at an Ivy League school, she had no qualms.

In his room, Ethan grabbed the suitcase he hadn't even unpacked from his stay at Olivia's to repack it with fresh clothes. Tossing it on the bed, he unzipped it and dumped the contents out, sifting through it to grab his toiletries. In one of the folded shirts, something caught his eye. A small framed painting had been tucked inside.

He picked it up and ran his thumb along the frame, admiring the skill of the artist in capturing the warm feeling of the Christmas tree lighting in Holly Wreath. Closing his eyes, he remembered how bitterly cold it was that night, but holding Olivia under the blanket, he had known then and there that they had a connection. Olivia had gone on stage and performed so beautifully, sharing a piece of herself with the town, and somehow, she had worried that it wouldn't be enough. She was a conundrum, and he wanted to spend as much time as she'd let him figuring her out. If he was lucky, that might be for the rest of their lives.

He turned the frame over and found a brief note from Olivia scrawled on the back that made him laugh and miss Olivia all the more.

Thank you for not walking away when I slammed the door in your face. This year's Christmas has been so much merrier because of you. Thank you for reminding me of the joy to be had at this time of the year. To love and be loved is the greatest gift I could have ever wished for, and you've given it to me.

Love,

Olivia

A knock at the door interrupted his thoughts. Still holding the watercolor to read and reread what Olivia had written, he answered the door, expecting to have Emma there, offering him more advice that she'd forgotten to give him earlier. He nearly dropped the gift from Olivia when he came face to face with Mallory.

"What are you doing here?" Ethan said, put off that she hadn't listened to him when he'd told her repeatedly that things were done between them.

"Can I come in?"

Ethan's first inclination was to send her on her way, but her countenance was penitent. She wasn't her usual bubbly self, laughing and flirting and flaunting.

RACHAEL ELIKER

"For a few minutes," Ethan said, stepping back and allowing her to enter. "I'm getting ready to go on a trip."

"To Holly Wreath?" Mallory asked as she adjusted her purse strap over her shoulder.

"Yeah. How'd you know?"

Mallory walked a few steps farther into the apartment, the click of her heels echoing in the empty spaces. "I saw the way you looked at her, Ethan."

"At who? Olivia?"

"Yes," Mallory swallowed. "That's why I came over."

Ethan closed his eyes and shook his head. "Mallory, you're not making any sense."

"No, I don't suppose I am," Mallory said. Her hands fidgeted with the clasp of her purse, and she cleared her throat. "I came over to apologize."

"Oh, yeah?" Ethan said. "What for?"

"For Derek. For hurting you. For giving you a hard time at the Holly Wreath Inn. I think I was jealous that it was so obvious what you two had together that I was being petty and childish, wanting it to be difficult for you. That was wrong of me."

Ethan was surprised by Mallory's confession, but he held no ill will toward her. "I appreciate that, and I accept your apology."

Mallory slouched down into the black leather couch in the middle of his living room, a mountain of her guilt replaced by relief. "Thanks. That's been a weight on my shoulders ever since I screwed up with Derek. I think deep down, I knew you and I weren't truly in love. Not that it's really a good excuse for what we did."

"How's he doing, by the way? After he stole my fiancée and all." Mallory smiled along with him when she realized Ethan was only teasing.

"I don't think he knew what he was getting into with me."

190

"That bad, huh?"

"I kind of chewed him up and spit him out. It might take a while for him to recover," Mallory said nonchalantly.

Ethan couldn't hold back a howling laugh. "Guess it serves him right."

"He definitely needs to earn his way off Santa's naughty list with some serious reflection and changing his ways, but at least now he realizes he's been bad. If he keeps acting the way he does, he's going to burn through all his friends and end up alone."

Ethan smiled. "I guess in a roundabout way, I'm glad you taught him a lesson."

Mallory smiled, but her eyes weren't as happy as her mouth was trying to be. She swallowed and pushed her red hair behind her ears, and clasped her hands together. "I'm also going to try to be better. After catching a glimpse of what you and Olivia had, I realized that I need to get my act together and find that for myself. No more party girl, no more breaking off engagements. I want a guy to look at me that way."

"What do you mean? You only saw Olivia and me together for about five minutes, and we were fighting the whole time."

"You were angry, yes, but there was such a real passion between you, and in all the years I've known you, I've *never* seen you happy about Christmas. I'm convinced any woman who can make you smile at Christmastime is your soulmate. You two are a cute couple."

"We are good together," Ethan agreed. "I hope things will work out for us. I'm needing a Christmas miracle to make it happen, I think."

"It will. You know how to woo women better than most." Mallory got up, swinging her purse as she strolled back to the door to let herself out.

Leaning on the open door, Ethan asked, "How did you find out where I was anyway? I only told my secretary, and as far as I know, only Emma was able to weasel it out of Peg."

Mallory shrugged. "Some girls in Holly Wreath put their selfies with you on social media, and they began trending. It was only a matter of time before one with a pinned location came up."

A throaty laugh escaped Ethan. "I have to give you credit for that. How clever of you."

Mallory lifted one shoulder and let it fall. "I'm not as dumb as people sometimes think."

"You're extremely smart, Mallory. Don't let anyone tell you otherwise."

Mallory chuckled, wiping at a tear that threatened to splash down her cheek. "I hope you get to see Olivia soon."

"I'm planning on it. I'm going to win her back by Christmas Eve if I have my way."

Worry changed Mallory's expression. "Haven't you heard?"

Ethan's heart lurched in his chest. "Heard what?"

"That whole area is about to be hit by a blizzard," Mallory said. "If you're wanting to see her for Christmas, it really is going to take a miracle."

CHAPTER 18

"Mom? You're staring out the window again," Heather said, entering the kitchen from her bedroom hallway. "Are you okay?"

Olivia tried to smile but was sure it looked pathetic, so she gave up altogether. "Of course. Yeah. Just washing some of these dishes after all the baking we did for tomorrow."

"Do you need help?"

Her smile at her daughter was genuine. "That's got to be a first. You asking to help with dishes? You hate doing the dishes even more than folding laundry."

"Consider it my Christmas present to you."

"Deal."

Olivia plunged a glass baking pan into the sudsy water and let it soak while she started washing a large mixing bowl. Heather rinsed and dried it, then hopped off her step stool to put it on the lazy susan.

They worked in silence for a few minutes, enjoying the Christmas music playing on Olivia's phone. As much as she wanted it to brighten her mood, there was still a gaping hole within that seemed as though it would never be filled again.

"Mom," Heather said, not meeting her in the eye, "I miss him."

Olivia pretended ignorance. "Him, who?"

Heather gave her a massive sassy eyeroll. "You know who. *Ethan.*"

Olivia finished the last cookie sheet and unstoppered the drain, rinsing out the washcloth and draping it over the side. "I'm sorry."

"I know he wasn't here very long, but things felt different in our house when he was here," Heather said. When she finished drying, she snuck a piece of peanut brittle from a cookie tin, though Olivia didn't stop her. "You were happy for the first time in a long time."

"I'm happy," Olivia said.

"I think you pretend to be happy for me because you don't want me to worry, but I can see things."

"See things? Like what?"

Heather said, "Like when you smile. When Ethan was here, I could see your smile in your eyes. Now when you do it, it's only your mouth. It looks all wrong."

Olivia swallowed the lump in her throat, knowing Heather was right. She'd felt like an empty shell since she'd sent Ethan away and had spent several sleepless nights wishing she could have redone the way she'd reacted to finding out about him being a billionaire. And why had it shocked her so much that he'd had a fiancée before her? She was a divorcee and surely didn't want men running the other direction because her marriage had crumbled.

"I'm sorry, honey. I'll try to do better," Olivia said, taking a chunk of peanut brittle for herself.

"I don't think you should try to do better. I think you and Ethan should make up."

Olivia chuckled softly. "I don't think it's that easy."

"Why?"

"Why? For one, I wasn't particularly kind to him when I found out who he was. Making up is contingent on us both being willing to forgive."

"Have you even asked? I know you have his phone number."

"No. I've been trying to work up the courage. I'm a bit of a coward, especially when I know I'm wrong."

"He'll forgive you. He loves you as much as you love him. Maybe more."

"More than me? How do you figure?"

"He did get you a new roof," Heather laughed.

Olivia shook her head, wondering when her daughter had become so mature and intuitive. "It's still not that simple."

"What's not?"

"Him," Olivia said as she absentmindedly played with her earring. "Us. Our lives are too different. I'm not sure I could ever mesh into his world, and I don't always want to feel like I'm being a burden on him because I'm not his equal."

Heather creased her nose, and Olivia knew what she'd said had sounded ridiculous. "You don't want to be together with him because he has a lot of money? That's dumb, Mom."

Olivia huffed. "Probably. But it's how I feel."

Heather was quiet for a moment as her brown eyes studied Olivia's face. "You're the one always telling me that money isn't what makes people happy."

"That's true," Olivia murmured.

"You know what I think the richest thing is?"

"The richest thing? Are you talking about gold versus diamonds? Stuff like that?"

Heather shook her head. "No. The richest thing is love. A lot of people love you, and that makes you just as rich as Ethan."

Olivia smiled through tears that had begun to accumulate

along her lower lashes, and she had to blink them away. "That's very insightful of you."

"So, does that mean you'll call Ethan?"

Olivia laughed and stroked her fingers through Heather's hair. "Sometime."

"Soon?"

"Yes. Soon."

"Good," Heather said. Perking up, she asked, "Can I watch a movie? I haven't seen *The Grinch* yet this year, and I always watch it before Christmas."

"Then you'd better go turn it on. It's going to be Christmas in about five hours."

Heather skipped away, stopping in the doorway to ask, "Are you coming?"

"In a minute. Just want to put a lid on all these goodies so I don't eat them before Christmas tomorrow."

"Can we have popcorn and M&M's while we watch the movie?" Heather pushed out her lower lip and looked at Olivia with puppy dog eyes.

"Sure, why not?"

Olivia moved around the kitchen, finishing her work and mulling over the sage advice her daughter had offered. It may have been an oversimplification of the situation, but then again, Olivia was probably making it more challenging than it needed to be. Just pick up the phone, dial his number, and apologize.

But first, she needed to talk to Twila.

Twila's phone rang twice before she picked up. "Are you out of sugar? Because I have a whole container over here just waiting to be turned into your toffee."

"No, I had enough of a stash over here to feed a small country. All my treats are made for tomorrow."

"Then what can I do for you?"

"Want to come over and watch a movie with us? I'll reheat

some enchiladas for dinner, although I'm feeling pretty lazy and imagine Heather will just eat popcorn for her meal."

"You don't have to ask me twice," Twila said. "Be over in a minute."

Olivia started the popcorn and felt her heart beating a little faster. If she was going to apologize to Ethan, she figured she better start with Twila.

"Smells divine in here," Twila said, letting herself in and hanging her coat over the back of the chair.

"It's all sugar and butter and chocolate. Not a salad in sight today."

Twila shrugged. "'Tis the season. That's what New Year's Resolutions are for, anyway."

Olivia laughed, glad her relationship with Twila hadn't been permanently tarnished by her selfish and mean words. Finishing off the popcorn on the stove, she dumped it into a large bowl and tossed it with a sprinkling of salt. Twila offered to carry the bowl for her so Olivia could climb onto the step stool to reach the candies in the top of her pantry. Tossing them over to Twila so she could climb down, Olivia took a deep breath to prepare herself.

"Twila, I really need to apologize to you."

Blinking once, the wheels turned in Twila's mind. "About what?"

"Because I was rude to you this past weekend. When you were trying to calm me down and offer advice about Ethan. I about bit your head off."

"Oh, that?" Twila batted her hand in the air. "Water under the bridge."

Ethan had said the same thing to Olivia when she'd been rude to him the morning of the gift delivery, and Twila's use of the expression seemed more than coincidence. It somehow had the power to lessen the weight off her shoulders and some of the worry off her mind. "Thanks for being so understanding. I didn't mean to snap at you the way I did, but I was feeling a bit...*emotional* at the time."

"Understandable. That was a shock to find out Ethan Wilder was *the* Ethan Wilder. I *knew* I recognized his face. Just couldn't remember from where. It's not every day I meet someone who I've only seen on magazine covers and television."

"Yeah, who knew he'd be escaping his life by coming to little old Holly Wreath?"

"Stumbling into town is more like it. I'm just sorry you found out the way you did. If I didn't get so darn excited about meeting a celebrity, you might not be in this pickle."

"That's unfair to put any of the blame on you," Olivia said. She filled up a water glass for herself, and the two of them shuffled to the living room where Heather was waiting at the ready to start the movie. "I feel like the common denominator in his situation. I overreacted."

Twila handed over the popcorn to Heather and plopped down next to her. "If there's one thing I know, it's that nobody's perfect. He should've said something, and you shouldn't be so afraid that every man who loves you is going to disappoint you."

Olivia sat down in a recliner, rocking herself as she nodded. "That's a difficult thing to get over."

"Undoubtedly. Just make sure you don't pass up a good thing because of fear," Twila said.

Heather shoved a handful of popcorn in her mouth. "That's what I've been trying to tell her."

"Manners," Olivia said and Heather closed her lips.

Twila chuckled and pulled Heather's head onto her shoulder. There was a glimmer in her blue gray eyes, and she said to Olivia. "Things will work out. You'll see."

Olivia pulled a knit blanket onto her lap, wishing she was

snuggling up with Ethan. "Someday, I hope I have as much faith as you."

"It's alright to lean on others once in a while," Twila said, reaching over to the popcorn bowl. "First though, you have to believe that you really are as wonderful as people think you are. When you can love yourself, you can let others love you."

Heather pointed the remote at the television. "Are we done talking? If we are, I'm going to push play."

Olivia smiled. "You're right. Better get started watching the movie, or we'll be up too late for Santa to squeeze down our chimney with presents."

Heather smacked her forehead with her hand and groaned. "Mom. I'm not a little kid anymore, remember?"

"Yeah, well, it's still fun to pretend. Now press play. I'm ready."

Through the whole movie, the weight of Olivia's phone on her lap was a reminder that nothing was going to change unless she made an effort. Every time she worked up the courage to pick up her phone, she caught Twila and Heather watching her, making her chicken out and check the weather instead. Holly Wreath was expecting a storm that would bring them a fresh layer of powdery white snow for Christmas. Out one of the windows in the dining room, Olivia could see feathery white flakes already falling.

When *The Grinch* finished, Heather begged to watch *The Polar Express*. After a day of cooking and cleaning for the cowboy who'd been staying at the inn since the day after Ethan left, not even the promise of her weight in chocolate could move her from her comfortable spot. She nodded sleepily at Heather who squealed with joy and started it. Olivia barely made it fifteen minutes into the movie before her eyes slid shut.

"Olivia?" Twila's voice sounded far away, and it took great effort to lift her eyelids.

Hmm? Is the movie over?

"Yep. It's after midnight, so let me be the first to wish you a Merry Christmas."

"Merry Christmas to you, too." Sitting her chair up, she looked around. "Where's Heather?"

"I sent her off to get ready for bed. I told her Santa couldn't deliver her presents until she was asleep, and she just rolled her eyes." Twila folded up the blanket Olivia had been using while Olivia put her arms high above her head and stretched through her back. "Your hunky cowboy guest arrived a little after eleven, and he went up to bed. He said not to wait up for him in the morning."

"Yeah, Rudger told me he has plans for Christmas."

"You know," Twila said, nudging her in the side. "If things don't work out with Ethan, you might consider seeing if Rudger is available."

Olivia grinned. "He's very polite, and I'll give you that he's handsome, but he's already spoken for."

"Not surprising, I suppose."

Twila bundled up and left for her house while the snow fell in droves. With the house silent and still, Olivia set out the few gifts she'd purchased, arranging them under the tree and putting handfuls of chocolates into the stockings, and candy canes on the tree. When she turned off the overhead lights in the living room, she leaned against the wall and admired the beauty in front of her lit by the warm glow of the Christmas tree. It wasn't extravagant or picture perfect, but it was home.

Checking her phone, there were no new messages, she regretted that she'd procrastinated so long that it was too late. She resolved to send him a text first thing in the morning as a peace offering. It seemed fitting to offer that as a gift to Ethan when she had nothing else to give.

For the first time since she'd argued with Ethan, she'd slept without tossing and turning. When she opened her eyes the next morning, she rolled over and reached for the blinds. The storm had blown through, and everything was sunny and covered in sparkling, pearl white snow. It was the latest Heather had ever let her sleep Christmas morning, and after eight uninterrupted hours of sleep, Olivia felt like she could conquer the world.

First, she had to keep the promise she'd made last night.

Her phone was charging on her nightstand, and when she turned it on, she was surprised to find a text message waiting for her. It was from Ethan. Her pulse picked up, and she knew she was smiling stupidly even before she read it.

Merry Christmas, Olivia.

Three simple words, and all her fears and apprehensions melted away like snow in the spring.

She texted back:

Merry Christmas to you, too.

It wasn't long before an answer came:

I'm sorry for last weekend.

Olivia wished she was looking at him face to face, but she'd take any form of communication she could get. She typed:

Me, too. I miss you. Think we can we give it another shot?

Her hands trembled while she waited for his answer. It all came down to his response, whether or not she'd completely destroyed any second chance they might have. Her phone dinged, and she read the message:

You've given me the one Christmas gift I really wanted.

Olivia wanted to jump off her bed and dance around the room, shouting with joy, but she didn't want to wake anyone who might still be sleeping. With her cheeks hurting from how widely she smiled, she texted back:

I wish we could have spent Christmas together.

Ethan texted back immediately:

That would make Christmas perfect, wouldn't it?

Olivia heard the doorbell chime. Rudger must've gotten locked out, and the last thing she wanted to do was freeze him out on the porch. Olivia wriggled into a pair of jeans and a sweater, then smoothing her hair into a ponytail, she tucked her phone into her back pocket. She wasn't done talking to Ethan.

Olivia felt like she was floating as she rushed down the hallway to the door. In the living room, Heather was quietly reading on the couch, and Twila had come over, and was stoking the fire with a new log.

"Didn't the doorbell ring?" Olivia asked.

"It did," Heather said, barely looking up over the top of her book.

Olivia stopped, wondering why everyone was behaving so oddly. "Why didn't you get it?"

Heather put her book down on her lap. "One of your house rules is that I'm not supposed to answer the door."

"And I was in the middle of getting the fire stoked," Twila said. "I was going to get it once I set down the logs."

"Ah," Olivia said, tugging at the bottom of her sweater. "I'd better get it before Rudger freezes. I haven't had a chance to shovel the snow off the porch and walkway yet."

At the front door, Olivia could see the silhouette of Rudger holding an armful of boxes. What he was doing with them at her house she couldn't guess.

Swinging the door open, her jaw dropped.

Smiling at her behind a stack of wrapped presents wasn't Rudger.

It was Ethan.

CHAPTER 19

The look on Olivia's face was priceless. "What? How did you? When?"

"Like I said, Christmas would be perfect if we were together, so I decided to make it happen."

Closing her eyes, she dropped her face into her hands. "I can't believe it."

Ethan was worried she was about to cry, and he put down all the gifts to free up his arms. "Hey. What's the matter?"

Olivia moved her fingers, and though her eyes were glossy with tears, she wasn't sad. Grinning widely, she said, "Nothing. Everything is absolutely perfect."

"Good. Because it's freezing out here. Can we come in?" Ethan asked.

Olivia helped Ethan pick up the gifts. "We?"

Out from behind the bush, Emma popped up, holding her arms over her head. "Tada! I knew you all probably missed me, so Rob and I tagged along with Ethan so we could all spend Christmas together."

"Rob came?" Olivia asked. "I'm so excited to meet him!" Unable to see him, Olivia asked, "Where is he?"

"Right here," Emma said, jabbing her thumb behind the bush.

Grabbing Rob's hand, Emma grunted and tugged, struggling to get her husband out of the snow drift where he'd sunk in. Losing her footing, she slipped and toppled back on top of him, laughing and shrieking as they flailed helplessly together.

"Help!" Emma cried. "I've got snow down my shirt!"

Twila and Heather came to see what all the commotion was, and when Heather saw who it was, she whooped and shouted, "Finally! You guys made it."

"You knew they were coming?" Olivia asked.

"Well, yeah. We had to coordinate," Heather said with a shrug. "Me and Ethan are getting pretty good at arranging surprises."

"I guess," Olivia said, wondering if she wasn't still dreaming.

Twila and Heather dragged the presents inside while Ethan and Olivia helped Rob and Emma wriggle out of the snow. Once free, everyone rushed inside, stomping off the snow, and shedding their coats. In the living room, Heather had piled the presents together, and the fire Twila had started was roaring, warming the room nicely.

"How'd you manage to get here?" Olivia asked. "The blizzard that blew through here last night was a monster."

"Tell us about it," Emma said. "I'm not the kind of person that gets uptight about traveling in adverse weather, but I think I bit off all my nails traveling yesterday."

"Did you fly in?" Olivia asked, sitting down on the couch next to Ethan, but not settling in completely.

"Partly. The airport in Holly Wreath closed before we could land, so we had to go south to an airport in Colorado, then pick up a truck that could make it through the snow," Ethan said. "We only got stuck a couple of times."

Olivia gasped, covering her mouth. "I can't believe you were out in that storm."

Ethan scooted closer on the couch and took his hand in hers. "It was worth it."

All eyes were expectantly on them, and the conversation hit a lull while everyone stared.

Not wanting an audience, Olivia spoke at the same time as Ethan. "Can we talk in the kitchen?"

"Whoa," Heather said. "You guys are on the same wavelength."

Laughing, Olivia pushed a stray lock of hair behind her ear and rose from the couch, leading the way. "Heather? You want to come and get some of the treats we made to share until I can get breakfast ready?"

Heather didn't have to be asked twice, and she rushed ahead of her mom and Ethan to take the food out to the rest of their guests. Stacking the tins so high she had to keep them from falling by tucking them under her chin, she stopped by Ethan.

Holding out her hand, Heather gave Ethan a fist bump. "Glad you're back."

Ethan touched his knuckles to hers. "This is the kind of Christmas miracle I can believe in."

Heather left, giving Olivia and Ethan the privacy they needed to say what was on their minds, but neither of them seemed to be able to figure out what they wanted to say. Ethan walked over to the counter and leaned against it, stretching his long legs out and crossing one ankle over the other the way he'd done so many other times while he had watched Olivia cook.

Knowing she was wasting time, she gathered her courage and spoke while she looked out the window at a blue jay that was helping itself to her birdfeeder. "Ethan, I think I need to be the one to apologize."

She looked to his face to see if he was giving away any of his thoughts through his expression. His hazel eyes were soft and gentle, and the corner of his lips were curled into the beginning of a smile.

He cleared his throat. "You can't heap all the blame on yourself. I certainly don't."

"I feel awful for what I did. It was in the heat of the moment kind of reaction, but when I calmed down to think it over, I could definitely see why you hesitated."

Ethan nodded. "Sure, but I also shouldn't have been hiding that part of me from you. I want to be able to share everything with each other. That's the kind of relationship I'm hoping for. One where we don't hold anything back."

Olivia swallowed. "I'd like that."

"If my having money does bother you, I'll keep gifts to a minimum and nix the extravagances. We can pretend that part of me doesn't exist."

"Heather reminded me of something yesterday," Olivia said, shifting on her feet and playing with the cuffs of her sweater sleeves.

"Oh, yeah? What was it?"

Olivia licked her lips and glanced behind her at the sound of laughter coming from the living room. "She reminded me that the richest kind of wealth is that of people who love and care about you. So if we look at it that way, I'm as well off as you are."

Ethan agreed. "I like that. I know for me, I've never been happier than when I knew I had your love. I'd trade all my worldly possessions to know you were mine."

A blush warmed Olivia's cheeks, and she looked shyly at him through her lashes. "That won't be necessary. My love is yours already."

Her words encouraged Ethan, and he stepped over to her, looping an arm around her waist. Hooking his finger under her chin, he brought her face up so he could look her in the eyes.

"There's something I need to tell you," Ethan said.

"Let me guess. You're secretly a spy, aren't you?" Olivia teased.

Laughter rumbled from Ethan, and he raised an eyebrow. "Wouldn't you like to know?"

Olivia shrugged and reached her arms up to clasp her hands behind his neck. "If you are, I want you to take me on some of your exotic trips once in a while, when I can get away from the inn and Heather has some time off of school."

"Done," Ethan conceded. "Although, I sometimes take trips to exotic destinations just for fun, too. No work involved."

"Sounds incredible," Olivia said while she played with the hair at the nape of his neck. "So, what's your secret?"

Ethan gave her his most dashing grin. "You're the most beautiful woman I've ever seen, and I've thought that ever since I met you at the diner."

"I thought you were too distracted by the diner food to notice little old me."

"You even outshined that," Ethan said, laughing as Olivia slugged him in the arm.

When Olivia's face went serious, Ethan stood at attention, waiting to hear what she had to say. "While we're sharing secrets, I have one."

"Do you, now?" Ethan said. "Shoot."

"I don't like chocolate covered cherries. I think they're gross."

Ethan laughed louder. "Then I guess one of *my* secrets is that I like them because I think they're *delicious.*"

Olivia made a face and pretended to gag, and Ethan threatened to tickle her if she kept it up. They laughed until neither of them could breathe, and they were leaning against each other for support.

Wiping a happy tear from her face, Olivia asked, "Anything else you want to confess while we're coming clean with each other?"

Ethan softened again, and his eyes trailed down to her lips. He would have loved to be kissing them, but there were some things that needed to be said beforehand.

"There are a million things I want to tell you about me, but that'll take time. I'm in no rush. There will always be something else new we're finding out about each other. You may think you're easy to read, but in the short time I've been with you, I've come to know you're full of mysteries. I can't wait to discover every single one of them, even if it takes a lifetime."

"I've been thinking the same thing. Why am I in such a hurry to rush through things with you?"

"Exactly," Ethan said, brushing her hair off her forehead. "What I want is for this to be considered a fresh start, and from now on, I want it to be clear with you about everything, starting with the fact that I absolutely adore you." Ethan rested a hand on her cheek and she smiled lovingly at him. "I didn't realize that I needed rescuing until I met you. Your goodness, your ambition, your vulnerability, and your simultaneously quiet but strong ambition inspire me to be the best man that I can be."

"I want to be all those things for you," Olivia said. Her chin was so cute as it trembled with another swell of happy tears.

"You are. In the few short weeks I was here, I saw you serving and sharing your gift for the violin with the town, even though it stressed you out so much you could barely remember the day of the week or your daughter's name. It was a testament to me when Heather, Twila, and I started planning for your roof renovation. So many people showed up and wanted to help because you're such a staple of Holly Wreath. You and your hot chocolate."

Olivia giggled. "You love me for my hot chocolate?"

"I'm not sure how you don't have guys lined up down the street when they get a sip of it," Ethan said, drawing her in closer.

"I'm very selective of whom I share it with."

"Then I'll consider myself someone special," Ethan said.

Olivia stood on her tiptoes, ready to brush her lips across his. "You are."

Inches away from what was sure to be a fantastic makeup kiss, a triumphant whoop from Heather interrupted them. Both their heads snapped over to the doorway where everyone else at the inn had snuck down the hall to spy on them.

Ethan reached for the hand towel hanging on the stove and chucked it toward his sister. "Way to ruin a moment."

Emma pointed to herself. "Hey, don't blame me. Heather's the one who couldn't keep quiet."

"Was not!" Heather cried shrilly. "Is it a crime now to be happy for my mom?"

"Hardly," Twila laughed, "but you were about dying of anticipation in the living room, salivating over all those presents, too. You have zero self-control."

"And is it wrong to want to open them to see what Santa brought?"

Olivia raised an eyebrow. "I thought you didn't believe in Santa anymore."

"I don't, but that doesn't mean I don't want to see what you and Ethan got me. I can play along with the spirit of Santa with the rest of you," Heather said. Wiggling in her spot, she asked, "Can we open them now? I see at least seven with my name on it."

Olivia glanced apologetically at Ethan, but he only smiled. "We'd better not keep her waiting. There are some really fantastic gifts in there, if I do say so myself."

"I bet there are," Olivia said.

Everyone turned to follow Heather, who bolted down the hallway and almost skidded past the living room as she slid on her socks. Ethan and Olivia followed last, with his arm draped across her shoulders. She reciprocated and hugged herself close to him with an arm around his waist, and it felt so right to Ethan to have her tucked up next to him.

Heather handed out the presents while the adults crammed together on couches and chairs, laughing as they talked and exchanged stories of Christmases past and *ooo*-ed and *ahh*-ed as they unwrapped gifts.

"This one's for Olivia," Ethan said, handing over a festive green bag tied together with red ribbon.

"What is this all about?" Olivia asked with a curious smile. "I think I've already gotten enough."

"Think of it as a gift for me, too," Ethan said.

"A gift for us both?" Olivia asked, stopping after she undid the ribbon and pulled out the first piece of tissue paper.

"Yeah. I'll benefit from it as much as you," Ethan said.

Sitting on the edge of his seat, he squeezed Olivia's hand in anticipation. Her smile betrayed her excitement, and she pulled out the rest of the tissue paper, then tipped back and clapped her hand over her mouth as she giggled.

"This is perfect," Olivia said, smiling ear to ear.

"Well," Heather said, impatiently bouncing in her seat on the floor, "what is it?"

Olivia pulled out her gift. "A book of classical violin music."

"I admit this gift isn't totally selfless. I'm looking forward to hearing you practice for me," Ethan said, kissing the crown of her head.

"I appreciate it," Olivia said, running her hand across the cover. "You'll get a personal violin recital anytime you want."

With the gifts disappearing under the tree, Olivia hugged the music book to her chest, watching the scene unfold with a grin on her face.

"What's so funny?" Ethan asked.

She leaned over and put her head on his shoulder. "Not funny. Just...incredible. This is how Christmas is supposed to be."

"I was thinking the same thing," Ethan murmured.

With the presents gone, Olivia stood. "Since there are a few more people here this morning than I was expecting, I'm going to go whip up some breakfast casserole and French toast."

"I'll help," Ethan offered, taking her hand and letting her guide him down the hallway.

In the kitchen, Olivia slipped on her favorite frilly apron and got out the mixing bowls. Ethan knew he should offer to stir something, but he was mesmerized watching her work. He'd been saving another special gift for her, and it felt like the perfect time to give it.

"I have something else for you," Ethan said, taking out the envelope from his back pocket. "I didn't want to make a big deal of it in there with everyone else."

Olivia dusted off her hands and planted her fists right above her hips. "Haven't you showered me with enough gifts? I'm already as happy as a hound dog on a scent."

Ethan smiled and laughed. "Let me guess. One of your grandpa's sayings?"

Olivia stuck out her tongue at Ethan. "Have you ever seen a hound chasing something? There's little in this world that exceeds that kind of joy."

"I believe you."

"My concern is you're going to give me a big head if you keep giving me everything my heart desires."

"Oh, that's hardly possible. I like to think of it as pampering. Tomorrow when Christmas is over, we can go back to all your backbreaking labor, but today, humor me."

Olivia chewed the inside of her cheek. "Alright. I'll play your little game."

Ethan handed over the envelope with trembling hands. He could hardly wait to see her reaction, and he hoped his gesture wasn't too much.

She tore open the envelope and started sifting through the papers that had been folded neatly inside. Her blue eyes flew up to his. "What is this?"

"It's the deed to your house."

Olivia's whole body began to shake, and Ethan was sure she was about to sink to the ground until he rushed forward to support her. Chuckling tightly, he said, "Easy there. Do you need to sit?"

"Ethan, you can't. It's too much."

Ethan's heart shot into his throat. "If you really don't want me to, I won't, but I'm going to have to insist. It's not so much that I wanted to give you something that would show the depth and breadth of my affection for you."

A tear slipped down Olivia's cheek. "Then what is it?"

Ethan tightened his hold around Olivia to keep her on her feet. "I wanted to give you peace of mind, to be able to unload some of the burdens that you've been carrying for so long. Without mortgage payments, it'll free up your funds to finish the renovations on your own, just like you wanted. Oh!" Ethan pulled out the keys to the truck they drove from his pocket. "This is yours, too."

Olivia just stared. "Keys? To what?"

"The truck we brought. You're going to need a vehicle

that can drive home all the supplies you're going to need to really make this house shine."

"A truck?" Olivia stuttered. "For me?"

Ethan jangled the keys. "Hope you like blue."

More tears poured out of her eyes, and she searched his face. "I don't have anything for you."

Ethan laughed, reassuringly rubbing her back. "You've given me more than I could have ever wished for. Happy memories to replace the pain of former Christmases, the possibility of a lifetime of happiness."

"You've given me the same thing, too," Olivia said. "I'm starting to feel we're a little uneven."

"Alright then. You want to know what you can do to make us even?"

"Anything," Olivia said.

"How about a mug of your hot chocolate? If I remember right, what a Holly Wreath Inn guest wants, a Holly Wreath Inn guest gets."

Olivia's smile matched his, and she draped her hands around the back of his neck. "Most definitely, but I think I can offer you one better."

"Yeah?"

Olivia stood on her tiptoes, her lips a few inches from Ethan's. Meeting his eyes, she asked, "Why don't I throw in a kiss?"

To continue with the series, *Christmas Kisses in Holly Wreath*, search for the title on Amazon.

OLIVIA'S SECRET HOT CHOCOLATE RECIPE

Cocoa Mixture
2 cups cocoa powder
3 1/2 cups granulated sugar
2 cups water
1 Tablespoon salt
Dash of cinnamon

Mix together ingredients in a saucepan and over medium-high heat, bring to 218-220F using a candy thermometer, stirring constantly. *Do not scrape the sides of the pan.* Chill overnight or minimum six hours.

Chocolate Cream
1 quart whipping cream
Chilled cocoa mixture

Whip cream until soft peaks form. Fold in cocoa mixture. Keep chilled until needed.

Steamed Vanilla Milk

2 gallons whole milk
2 1/2 Tablespoons vanilla extract

Heat milk until hot. Add vanilla.

To serve, mix one or two heaping spoonfuls of chocolate cream into a mug. Add hot vanilla milk and stir. Top with marshmallows or whipped cream, and sprinkle with crushed peppermint candies. Enjoy!

ABOUT RACHAEL

Humor. Romance. Happily Ever Afters. So much to write, so little time!

USA Today Bestselling Author Rachael Eliker is an avid reader and author with eclectic tastes, but as long as the story has humor, swoony romance, and maybe a horse or two, she's happy. When she's not writing, she's probably running lonely stretches of country road, riding her old horse, or working on a home improvement project. She enjoys passing the time with her husband and children on their Indiana hobby farm, having a good laugh, and making memories with friends and family most of all.

Learn more about Rachael Eliker and her upcoming works by visiting: www.RachaelEliker.com

MORE BY THE AUTHOR

Want more billionaires? Look for Rachael's new sweet romance series, To Love a Billionaire.

For a full list of Rachael's works, search for her on Amazon.

To leave a much-appreciated review for this book, please consider writing one on your preferred platform.

Made in the USA
Monee, IL
24 December 2022